SARAH

Johnny Fowler

Sarah © 2011 by John R. Fowler

ISBN-13: 978-1461066781
ISBN-10: 1461066786

This novel is a work of fiction. All of the events, characters, names and locales depicted in this novel are entirely fictitious, or are used fictitiously, though reference may be made to actual historical events or existing locations.

Other Books by Johnny Fowler

Mountain Woman
Panhandle Blizzard
Eclipse of the Heart
Treason at White Sands
Hidden Agenda
Kill Without Remorse
Love Walked In
Explosions of Fire
The Mercenary's Daughter
DEA Conspiracy
Diplomatic Immunity
Spanish Fly
Vengeance is Mine
Murder in the Loop

Mary Hardy Series
Hardy, Texas Ranger: The First Female Texas Ranger
Hardy, Texas Ranger: In Oklahoma Territory
Hardy, Texas Ranger: In the Davis Mountains
Hardy, Texas Ranger: In the Big Thicket

SARAH

Chapter 1

Sarah Nance agreed to attend the bank's Founders Day Picnic because her husband, Harold insisted. He claimed it would look bad if his wife didn't attend. "Please don't drink so much," she said on the drive to the park. "That would be much worse than me not attending with you."

He snapped back at her, rudely. "I never drink too much. You and those idiots at work keep saying I have an abuse problem. I can stop anytime I choose. An alcoholic can't. I don't want to hear another word about me. This is a fun time picnic and they'll have a keg or two. Everybody will be enjoying a couple of brews."

Neither spoke until they entered the park. She cringed back against the door, knowing what will happen and was already dreading the evening. Harold found a place to park, opened his door, and started walking toward the picnic area. She opened her door and hurried after him. "Please wait for me; don't leave me. I don't know many people since I see your fellow employees twice a year, here and at the Christmas party."

"Then come on," he said without looking back. "I see men already standing around the beer wagon."

He stopped at a table under a tree and gestured. "Wait here; what do you want to drink?"

"A diet coke or diet anything."

She watched him hurry to the beer wagon, reach for a twenty-ounce cup, and fill it with beer. He downed half, and then refilled it before picking up a can of diet coke from a vat of ice. When he reached her table, he put her drink down, and then poured half the cup of beer down his throat. She watched his throat bobble up and down as he swallowed.

"Please slow down, there's plenty of beer. I see another keg in the wagon."

With a scowl at her, he emptied the cup, turned without speaking, and went back for a refill.

Sarah sipped her coke and looked around. She recognized several faces, but couldn't remember their names. Resolved to sit here alone for the evening, she began people watching as a way to pass the time. She enjoyed seeing how they were dressed and acted.

Thankfully, it was a cool evening for the first day of May. Last year it had been extremely humid and hot. A nice breeze blew across Cyprus Creek.

Letting her mind wander, she had read that the bank opened its doors for business on the first day of May in eighteen-hundred sixty-one. This will be the hundred-fiftieth anniversary. Their advertisements always include the part about the Cyprus Creek State Bank as being the only bank owned by a local family for the entire time.

Sarah saw Harold talking with several men around the beer wagon and noticed him refilling his cup often. She shrugged her shoulders, resolved to the fact he would soon be drunk. What could she do? Other than make a scene and that would only increase his drinking. Every time she went out with Harold, it ended with him getting drunk. If he hadn't insisted, she wouldn't be here.

Her eyes moved around the crowd until she saw a group of men talking. One of the men was significantly taller. He was facing her. Something about him caused her to study him as her breath caught in her throat for a second. Long and lanky, she thought of Garry Cooper, the old western movie star.

She was studying his strong chin when their eyes met. Like a laser beam, his gaze penetrated her. She wanted to pull away, but her head wouldn't cooperate. A few seconds later, another man joined the group and he turned to speak. While she had the chance, she shifted her gaze away from him, but kept him in sight. Something about this man intrigued her.

When he finished talking with the new addition to the circle, his eyes returned to her. When he discovered her gaze had moved on, she detected a slight frown. With nothing better to do, she watched the tall man out of the corner of her eye, but never looking directly at him. The way he had locked on her with his eyes sent a pleasant thrill down her spine. Her heart missed a beat and her temperature raised a couple of degrees. This was a first and it scared her.

A few minutes later, she saw a busty redhead hurry to intercept him. He stopped to talk with her, and then moved on, leaving a very frustrated woman behind. The redhead put her hands on her ample hips and stomped her foot.

Sarah wanted to giggle; this was first amusing sight of the evening. Her smile faded when she looked back at Harold. He was still drinking beer as if it was his life's blood. She knew he wouldn't last much longer drinking so much, so fast. He ate a light lunch, but that wouldn't help with the volume he was consuming.

Drifting her eyes around the milling group of bank employees and their families, she again spotted the tall man. He was walking toward a stage where a band was busy arranging their instruments and speakers. He chatting with them a few minutes before a man Sarah recognized as the president of the bank walked to the stage. He stepped up and reached for a microphone. The tall man moved away from the stage and joined several men watching.

Mr. Boyd, the bank president, tapped the mike for attention. "Welcome, fellow employees of Cyprus Creek State Bank. It was one-hundred-fifty years ago today that our bank opened for business. Enjoy our annual Founders Day Picnic. The caterers have advised they're ready. Help yourselves to a fine dinner. There's steak, sausage, ribs, chicken and boiled shrimp. No calorie or carbohydrate counting is allowed today. The beer wagon is open for those that want a cold brew. There is a wine table adjacent to the serving table, as well as soft drinks, tea and lemonade."

Sarah watched the people began to form into four lines along two serving tables. All but one of the men at the beer wagon left to get in line. Harold was now seated at a table with two cups of beer in front of him. The other man filled a cup and hurried to join his wife, already in line saving him a place.

She hoped Harold would come to her, but that faded when she saw his face. He was past knowing anything, except how to drink.

Grinding her hands together, she debated her options, stay here and forego eating, join the line and fill a plate alone, or go to Harold and try to get him into their car."

A deep, but soft voice caused her to jump. The tall man was standing in front of her gazing down. "Harold's totally out of it," he said. He held out his hand, "Sarah, please join me for dinner. I'm afraid Harold is past the point of walking to the serving tables."

She wanted to reach for his hand, but held back. "I'm sorry, you know my name and my husband, but I don't think we've met."

"Gary Justice," he said, still offering his hand. "Now, can we go eat, I'm starved."

She reached for his hand, "It's nice to meet you, Mr. Justice. I guess I'm hungry, or I should be. I haven't eaten anything since toast and coffee for breakfast and that was hours ago."

He released her hand, but offered his arm. She put her hand on his elbow and he led the way to the serving table.

"Are you a bank employee?" she asked. "I haven't seen you before." She wanted to add that she would have remembered him, but held that back.

"In a way, yes, I'm associated with the bank." He motioned for a young man to come to him. Mr. Justice said, "Marvin, fill a plate with food, and take it to Harold Nance." He gestured toward the beer wagon.

"Yes sir," Marvin said. "What does he want?"

Gary turned to Sarah and waited for her to reply.

"Normally, he would choose steak, but I'm afraid he's past eating now. It appears that drinking beer is all he's interested in tonight."

Justice took it from there. "Then take him a variety, if

he's hungry, he can choose for himself. Make sure there's a nice piece of steak."

Marvin went to the other serving line and stood at the end.

"Thank you," she said, meaning it. "But as I said, Harold won't eat. He never does when he's drinking."

"I agree with you, but maybe he's not that far yet." He stepped back and let her go through the line first. She filled her plate with a modest amount of tossed salad and a few shrimp. As he filled his plate with steak and vegetables, he said, gesturing at her plate. "That wouldn't keep a bird alive."

"Of course not, but then not many birds eat salad and boiled shrimp."

He chucked, deep and hardy. She appreciated his joyful personality and ready smile. "You got me there, but please try the steak." He speared a piece of meat and put it on her plate. They picked up a glass of ice tea and he led her toward the tables. "I see a table with a man and two women. I suggest we join them to keep down small town gossip."

He asked, when they approached the table, "May Mrs. Nance and I join you?"

They all nodded. "Of course," one of the women said after hastily swallowing. "It looks like Harold is about to go down for the third time. That man, I've never seen anybody put down so much beer in such a short time."

Sarah blushed in spite of doing her best to let the remark about her husband slide. Thankfully, Gary came to her rescue. "Nothing but pleasant talk at the table, please," he said. He pointed at several ducks and geese on the water and told a funny story involving ducks.

Even Sarah had to laugh, in spite of her embarrassment about Harold. Gary followed with another story and kept the group entertained during the meal. His natural wit and humor a blessing.

He looked down at her plate and gave her a private wink. "Very good, you ate all the rabbit food and fish bait. Now do damage to the steak while I'm gone for desert. I see the others got theirs earlier. Do you want apple or peach cobbler?"

"Thank you, no, I'm full, or will be if I eat that steak."

He stood and walked toward the table for desert. When he came back, he placed a bowl of steaming apple cobbler with a large scoop of vanilla ice cream on top in front of her. She glanced up at him.

"A reward for finishing the steak and I would have felt guilty eating this with you sitting there without any. The cobbler is hot and the ice cream is melting. Get busy young lady."

She lifted her spoon and took a bite. It was delicious. They both ate it all. The others at their table had drifted away, leaving them alone.

The band started playing. As people finished eating, a few of the youngsters started a volley ball game. Several men were playing basketball. The older men formed teams for horseshoe pitching.

A few couples were on the dance floor. "May I ask how tall you are?" Gary said.

She met his face, "Five-ten without shoes. But if I may ask, why do you want to know that?"

"Will you dance with me? I hate to dance with a woman so short I have to bend over all the time."

"What a clever line, but a good one, it worked. I would enjoy dancing with you. I hate bending over to be shorter than the man I'm dancing with."

He chuckled and offered his arm.

She glanced at Harold. He sat at the table with two cups in front of him. "Somebody filled them," Gary said. "I don't think he could have managed. I see the plate of food is untouched."

"I know," she said. "Maybe I shouldn't dance and take him home."

"Nonsense, he's doing fine and not bothering anybody," he said. "Let him sit and drink those two. After what he's consumed, two more won't make any difference. Besides, why let him ruin your evening."

"I shouldn't, I want to dance. But, before we start, I must warn you, it's been ages. I'll be rusty. Harold never learned and refused to let me teach him."

"As they say, it's like riding a bike; it'll come back in a couple of minutes."

He took her into his arms and he felt good. His chest and stomach was hard and flat, and his shoulders broader than she had guessed. His feet moved with the grace of a professional dancer. He pulled her closer and her face fit beautifully along his neck. "Wonderful, perfect," he whispered into her hair. "I knew we would be right dancing together."

As he predicted, in less than a minute, she adjusted to his dancing style and together they floated around the floor. Her mind was on the music, and she was dancing with a handsome man, with a special feeling inside her.

Gary kept her on the dance floor for at least a dozen songs, and then, when a tune ended, Marvin tapped him on the shoulder. "Mr. Justice, it's time," Marvin said.

He frowned at the interruption, but said, "Thanks Marvin, I'll be there in a minute."

He led Sarah to the side of the floor. "Please wait for me."

"I will," she replied. She knew she should leave, but wouldn't since this was the first time in ages she was enjoying herself. She glanced around the gathering employees and saw the redhead giving her an evil eye. She wanted to chuckle, but held it in check.

Gary hurried toward the stage.

Thomas Boyd, the bank president was obviously waiting, holding the microphone. When he saw Gary approaching, he announced, "As I said, today we celebrate one-hundred-fifty years of continuous service to the citizens of Cyprus Creek and surrounding area towns. We now have twelve branch locations."

Boyd paused and glanced at Gary Justice before continuing. "What's even more remarkable, the Cyprus Creek State Bank has been owned by only one family. The current owner's great, great, grandfather opened the bank at its current location in 1861. Please welcome, Gary Justice."

Sarah gasped, startled. Gary stepped on the stage,

dressed more like a cowboy than the owner of a bank. The muscles on his arms and chest clearly visible through the blue knit shirt and the faded jeans outlined his muscular thighs. She wanted to giggle. She noticed he was wearing boots. Not that boots are uncommon, but the owner of a bank.

Gary took the microphone and faced the audience. "This is the first Founders Day Picnic I've had the pleasure of attending in years. I was away in college, and then the military. As you know, my grandfather passed away last February. My father is more interested in ranching than banking. So granddad passed the baton down to me."

A round of applause greeted him.

"Before granddad Justice died, he said one word more than once, continuity. I understood what he said for me to do, the original policies and mandates that have been passed down through three generations will continue. I'm not about to stumble now. Honesty, integrity, customer service, and above all, understanding of our customers' problems, needs, and helping solve, rather than contributing to their troubles is still our policy. Employees will be treated fairly and given the authority to excel at their assigned responsibilities. I'm not going to be a micro manager," he said with emphasis.

His eyes swept the faces watching him, but stopped for a second when they reached Sarah. "Continue to enjoy our special day; the band is ready to play again. Above all, have fun." His eyes remained on her as he finished his short speech.

He jumped from the stage and was greeted by a crowd of employees, wanting to shake his hand.

She giggled when she saw the redhead in his face, wanting to give him a hug. He escaped by turning to shake hands with several men, easing away from the brazen woman. He found Sarah, waiting, smiling, when he managed to escape.

She took his offered hand and walked with him to the dance floor, now filled with couples. "You own the bank?" she said, when she folded into his arms. "You can't be much older than me."

"I turned thirty about three weeks ago."

"I was right. May I ask a question?" she said.

"Of course, ask anything," he said with an encouraging smile.

"You said your father is alive and lives on a ranch."

She felt a slight shrug of his shoulders. "I suspect I know where you're going with that question. That's an easy enough question to answer. I've been asked many times. My father wasn't interested in the bank, he never was. He's a rancher through and through. I guess I got my grandfather and great-great grandfather's genes. I earned my bachelor and masters degree in finance and accounting. However, my father had some input; I also have degrees in animal husbandry and agriculture."

This man continued to amaze her. With each passing minute, her admiration for him increased. The way he handled himself and how he possesses the ability to ease stressful situations without hassle appealed to her.

"Now, Sarah," he said. "Tell me about you."

"Don't go to sleep listening to me. I'm the daughter of a public school couple. Mom teaches and Dad's the superintendent. We lived a few miles out of town, on a small acreage, we had a few cows, and goats when I was growing up. I have a bachelor and master's degrees in education. I teach the fourth grade. I met Harold in college. We married after I graduated. We have no children, by mostly my choice. He had a drinking problem back then. I thought it was only the college scene and I could change him. I was sure that having a wife and responsible job would help. That was a big mistake on my part. He only got worse."

"Enough of that," he put in. "Nothing negative will invade our pleasure of dancing and enjoying the evening. When it's time to go, I'll help you with Harold. Now we dance and laugh, nothing but fun."

If her feet ever touched the floor she wasn't aware of it. It felt as if her body were made of air. She wanted to float around the floor in his arms. Her mind at ease now, the awful situation with Harold could wait. As he said, dance, laugh and have fun and she was enjoying her time with Gary.

The band announced the last song of the evening. He

15

held her even closer. Her head on his shoulder, one strong hand on her back, the other clutching her hand, and she wanted the night to never end.

His lips were touching her hair, and he whispered with his lips almost touching her ear. His warm breath sent a shiver cascading down her spine. "I must tell everybody goodnight. Please go to your car and bring it to the gate the caterers are using. Drive as close to Harold as possible. I'll be there as soon as I can to help you get him in your car."

"That's not necessary, I can manage. I have before."

He was in a hurry. "Please, do as I asked. There's no way you can lift him. He passed out an hour ago."

She watched him hurry away. When she lost sight of him, she went to her car and sat for a moment reflecting on the situation. She spoke to the windshield as a thought entered her mind. "Has Gene has been seducing me?"

A giggle followed. No alarms or pangs of regret or guilt flashed. Her conscience was clear. With a smile on her face, she drove to the gate. Marvin waited and opened the metal gate for her and she stopped within a few feet of Harold and stepped out.

"Mr. Justice asked me to help with Mr. Nance. He said for us to wait for him."

Sarah nodded, her smile now gone as they walked to Harold. His head was on his chest. She lifted his face and saw his state; he was in an alcohol stupor. His eyes were unfocused and his lips sagged open.

She saw Gary coming, almost at a trot. "I got here as fast as I could." He looked at Harold and saw his condition, but didn't comment. "Sarah, open the car door. Marvin, take one arm, I'll have the other. Together, we'll lift him and put his arms on our shoulders and we can carry him to the car."

Sarah watched the two men lift Harold and put him in the front seat. Gary reached across and snapped the seat belt. "He'll be fine, drive carefully."

"Thank you, Mr. Justice. Marvin, I appreciate your help."

She nodded at the young man and smiled at Gary.

She drove through the gate and saw Marvin closing it behind her. On the drive home, she felt anger at Harold and growled. "I'm going to leave you in the car. I could shove you out on the lawn, but the neighbors would see you tomorrow morning. It'll be hot in the garage, but you deserve it. Hopefully, you'll sweat out some of the beer, but I hope you don't throw up in the car or wet your pants."

She turned into her driveway and noticed a car followed. Sarah looked back and saw Gary parking behind her. Another car parked in front of the house and Marvin jumped out.

Gary walked to the passenger side. "Sarah, open the front door and guide us to where you want Harold. Marvin and I'll carry him the way we did at the park." The two men put Harold's arms over their shoulders and pulled him into the house, his feet dragging. Sarah opened the door and waited in the hall. "In here," she said.

She hurried to pull the bedspread and sheet down. "Put him on the bed, I can manage."

Together, the two men put Harold's limp form on the bed. Gary stood and faced Marvin. "Thanks, I appreciate it. I'll see you Monday."

Marvin nodded toward Gary and Sarah and went out of the bedroom. Sarah followed and opened the front door. "Thank you, again," she said as the young man hurried toward his car.

She hurried back to the guest bedroom and saw Gary had Harold's shirt off and was working on his belt. She rushed to help. "I can do that," she said.

He ignored her and continued to undress Harold. Sarah wanted to help, so she removed his shoes, and then jerked the pants down when Gary lifted Harold's hips from the bed. She pulled the sheet up and they went to the door. She left the bathroom light on, but flipped the switch on the bedroom light and closed the door. If he woke, he would need the light to find the way to the bathroom, she hoped.

"I don't know what to say," she said. "Other than thank you."

"That's enough. Is there any coffee in the kitchen?"

"Of course, follow me. I can make a pot."

He sat at the bar and watched her. His long legs stretched out. She finished and sat across from him and met his gaze. "It'll be a few minutes," she said.

She put her arms on the bar, watching him. He reached across and covered her hands with his. "Sarah, we need to talk."

"I suspected that. You want to discuss Harold job performance."

"We do a routine employee evaluation each quarter. Harold has slipped down to the unsatisfactory level. His rejection ratio on his loan applications is double the next lowest. He has seven tardy occurrences the past two weeks."

She moaned, but wasn't surprised. "I leave at seven-forty in the mornings and make sure he's here at the bar eating breakfast before I leave. I know he'll oversleep if I don't make him get up."

"Then he went back to bed after you left," Gary said. "He always had an excuse, car trouble, traffic jam, sick, and so forth. Then his lunch hour has taken as much as two hours. One day, he didn't come back. I suspect he was in a bar."

She nodded and wasn't surprised.

"Now why I came to you tonight," Gary said. "Harold has used up his grace period. I'm going to meet with him on Monday at ten o'clock."

"I see," she said, her face strong, no visible sign of stress or surprise. "I've been expecting this. In fact, I'm surprised it took so long."

He was still holding her hands. "We try to be as lenient as possible, but there comes a time when actions must be taken. May I ask a few personal questions?"

"Of course, ask anything. I'll be honest and candid in my answers. I know you're trying to help me."

"Pour us a cup, and then I'll start on the hard part."

She stood and reached for two cups in the cabinet. "Cream or sugar?" she asked.

"Black," he said.

"I like coffee black as well." She placed two cups on the

bar and sat down, taking a deep breath. She was ready for the inevitable.

"Financially," he asked, "how are you?"

"With both of our salaries, we're doing fine, my car is clear, we're still paying on his, but it's down to three more payments. Of course, we have the house payments. I've managed to put back a little each payday. We have a C D at the bank, ten thousand."

"That's good to hear. Now, listen carefully. I can relate to what you're experiencing."

Surprise showed on her face, but she didn't comment.

He saw her expression and answered her unspoken question. My wife, Connie, was an alcoholic."

"What happened?" she asked.

"She was killed in a car crash. I took the keys away, but she had made a duplicate set I didn't know about. She hit a tree, no skid marks; her alcohol level was three times the legal limit. The police said she went to sleep or passed out. I suggest you take Harold's keys when he's drunk."

"I always drive when he's drinking. I've been worried about him."

"Good," he said. "Now, back to where I was going. When he's terminated, I suggest you have your money tied up where he can't get it. He may withdraw the entire balance and go on a binge. If he does, he'll be broke in a few hours, somebody will rob him or he'll blow it. I recommend you move the checking account and tie up the C D where he can't get his hands on it."

She took a swallow, thinking. "How do I do that? Both of our salary checks are automatically deposited to a joint account at your bank."

"It's going to take some paper work, but it could be worth it to you. I suggest using a different bank. Have your salary changed immediately, sent it to the new account, and move most of the money in your joint account. He could easily find your new account if you use our bank. When does the C D mature?"

"Soon, let me look." She went to the desk and opened an envelope. "May twenty," she said.

"If you want, let me handle that on Monday. I can make sure he can't turn it into cash."

"Please, but what about his salary?"

"I can't say for certainty, but I'll also look into that as well. There is also the matter of severance pay to consider. I'll take care of that as well, if you'll give me your new account number and the name of the bank. I'll have it deposited in your account. You can assume complete control of your financial obligations such as paying bills and the reoccurring loan payments."

"Why is that important?" she asked. "I take care of all the business now and pay the bills."

"To keep it safe of course, for both of you. If he reacts as I expect, he could blow every cent immediately. He will need help, or that is what I expect. From experience, when he gets the termination notice, the odds are Harold will go on a long drinking binge. Expect and prepare for the worst. If it doesn't happen, great, but if it does, you are protected."

"I understand about the money," she said. "Why are you doing this for me, for Harold and me?"

He finished his cup of coffee. She stood and refilled both cups, and then sat again. He reached across and covered her hands with his. His attention was welcome and appreciated.

"Sarah, I like you. That's no secret; we both know that. We felt it when we danced and now, holding your hands, it's even stronger. Harold's an employee. I'm going to do my best to make this as easy as possible for both of you."

They were both meeting the others gaze. "I don't want him to pull you down with him," he added. "I've seen this happen before. Before he hits bottom, he could crush you, physically, mentally, and financially."

He sipped the hot coffee before speaking again. "After Connie, I took several courses dealing with substance abuse. In my management courses, this problem was addressed many times. A common occurrence for personnel directors, both alcohol and drug abuse."

His hands were gentle and warm on hers. His face genuinely concerned. She trusted him, even though they had

20

known each other such a short time. "Please tell me everything I need to do. I'm embarrassed to say this, but I need help. There's nobody else for me to turn to."

"I will. When do you finish school for the year?"

"Our last day is on Friday, the twenty-first."

"That's three weeks from now," he said. "I'll postpone the meeting with Harold until you have time to take care of the financial matters. Instead of immediate termination, I'm going to demand he seek help. Legitimate help, such as a rehab center and counseling. I'll give him until the twenty-first to take action with positive assurance if he takes no action, he'll be dismissed. I predict one of two things will happen. He'll respond to my demand, or he'll twist off and hit the bottle. I hate to be a pessimist, but I expect the latter. Take care of your financial matters immediately. School will soon be out and you can better cope with the stress."

Her face reflected her concern. "How many times can I say, thank you?"

"None are needed. Together we can work through this."

He stood and walked toward the door, she stood to follow him. He stopped suddenly and reached for his wallet withdrawing a card and walked back to the bar and picked up a pin. He lined through a number and wrote another. He added three more. "The number I lined out was my office at the bank, but at the desk of my secretary. The number I put on the card is my private number, also my apartment, cell and the ranch. Nobody but me will answer these numbers. Call me anytime, day or night."

She took the card from him. Then picked up a scratch pad and wrote two numbers. "Here and my cell. I have free time from one to one-forty-five every day. My students go to music. I'm usually in the teacher lounge, but I'll have my cell. In the evening, I try to have dinner on the table by six. Then Harold goes to the den and opens a quart of beer. I go to my bedroom. I won't see him again until breakfast."

He looked at her with understanding. She wanted him to call, hopefully, as much as he wanted her to call him.

"He sleeps in the guest bed where he is now. That

started over a year ago. He was sick-drunk and I moved him to that bed. Sleeping with a drunk is awful. He moved his things the next day."

"I understand that. Connie lost all interest in anything except booze. "A hell of a way to live."

She followed him to the door, before he opened it; he turned and opened his arms for her. Without thought, she went to him and circled his neck with her arms and their bodies pressed together. His hand stroked her hair; the other hand pressed her closer. Her heart pounded as she meshed with him. Wanting him to continue his endearment with her. Her face burrowed into his shoulder while her fingers caressed his neck.

Finally, he stepped back and opened the door. She saw his face, a look of rapture, a look she never saw with Harold. She wondered what he saw as he scanned her face, but hoped her feeling were etched for him to read.

"Hang in there," he said, before he went out. "We'll work through this, and you can lean on me, please."

"I will. I'm not sure why you came to me, but again, thank you."

He was gone into the night. She watched until the taillights faded, and then went back inside. Almost in a trance, she turned the coffee off and washing the pot, and then went to her bedroom. Sarah took a quick shower and put her gown on and went down the hall and peeked in to check on Harold. He was asleep, his breathing regular.

With a groan, followed by a sigh, she went to her bed and lay down and turned the lamp off. A moment later, the phone rang. "I just got to my apartment," Gary said. "Is everything okay there?"

"Everything is fine. Harold's asleep and I was just lying down. Perfect timing on your call."

"It seems where you're concerned," he replied softly, "everything is perfect. Do you have anything planned for tomorrow?"

"I usually go to church. Harold will sleep until well after lunch. Then a few domestic chores, laundry and clean."

"Which church," he asked.

22

"Baptist, the one three blocks past our house."

"If your cousin happens to be in town, can he join you?"

She laughed when she understood his question. "Of course, cousin Gary. I would like that, a lot."

"Will it cause you a problem?" he asked. "I mean, with Harold should anybody recognize me."

"I doubt anybody will recognize you, but then a few members may be customers of your bank. Harold is extremely jealous. It could present a problem for me."

"Then, will you have lunch with me at a very private place where I know that nobody will see us?"

"That would be better for me," she said.

"Then, I'll meet you after church."

"I'll be looking for you," she said.

They both said, "Goodnight," and they hung up.

Her mind on Gary; she relaxed and pulled the other pillow into her arms.

Chapter 2

She carefully selected her dress. For the first time in ages, she wanted her appearance to be its best. The dress she finally settled on was blue with white accessories. She stood in front of the full-length mirror and examined herself. She felt alive this Sunday morning. Attending church alone had always been uncomfortable since Harold never went with her. The thought of meeting Gary for lunch afterwards worried her, but not enough to call and cancel.

On the drive to the church, she decided to skip church. She called Gary on his cell phone. "I decided not to attend church today," she said.

"Will you have still have lunch with me?" he asked.

"Yes, where shall I meet you?" she asked.

"I don't like to hide to see you," he said. "But for your sake and to prevent causing possible trouble for you in the future, it's best. The parking area behind the football stadium will be vacant on Sunday morning, and there are no houses or streets close."

"I'll meet you in about fifteen minutes," she said, nervously.

She entered the parking area and saw Gary standing beside his car. He was dressed in gray slacks with a black coat. His crisp white shirt and red tie caused her breath to catch in her throat. His sandy brown hair and masculine face appealed to her. She parked beside him and he opened her door.

"Beautiful," he said. "I love your dress. In fact, I love everything about you, your bright eyes and dancing blond hair."

"I like your selection of clothes," she said. "They are perfectly coordinated. But, then I liked you in jeans, a western shirt and boots."

"I think we make a handsome couple," he said. "No, scratch that, we make an attractive couple."

She glanced his way, only to see a thin smile and twinkling eyes.

"Follow me," he said.

"Where are we going?" she asked.

"I'm taking you to a very special place, home cooked food. It's very private and nobody will see us, I promise."

"Gary, are you sure? I mean, with Harold and my situation, the bank. Is this smart?"

"Probably not, but I want you to have lunch with me. You said Harold will be sleeping."

She gave him a smile of acceptance. She wanted to be with him. "Okay, but don't leave me hanging at a light."

"Not to worry, I won't. If you have to stop, I'll wait for you."

She had followed Harold and he never glanced back and it seemed he did his best to make lights on yellow. Such a difference. Gary treated her with respect. Harold treated her like an adversary and did things he knew would bother her. Such a difference, she thought.

Gary led her through a residential area and stopped at an apartment. He rushed back and opened her door. "Your apartment?" she asked.

"Our meal is in the oven," he said.

Again, she was concerned. The thought of going to his apartment disturbed her, but in a way, excited her. Her emotions and feeling for him were foreign, but she loved it.

He opened the door and she caught the smell of a roast. For a few moments, she wondered if he brought her here for something else besides lunch.

She stepped through the door and looked around and saw the typical efficiency apartment. He caught her glance. "It's a place to put clothing and sleep when I'm in town. I go to the ranch when I can. It's too far to commute every day."

He had mentioned a ranch before. "When you say ranch, do you mean your parents ranch?" she asked.

"Nope, mine. Part I bought, part I inherited from my grandfather, it joins my parents land, but separate. Well, we

25

help each other, but I have my cattle. The original house is on the part from my grandfather. He had the house built with native stone sometime in the twenties. I remodeled and modernized it, but some of the original furniture is still in the house. I can't wait for you to see it. It's western architecture, massively built, with a fireplace ten feet long. It opens into the living room and the master bedroom on the other side of the wall."

Unsure how to reply to his comment about her seeing it, she changed the subject. "Can I help with the meal?"

"No on helping, at least not in that beautiful dress. Except for a shirt, I have nothing for you to wear. I should have asked you to bring something. I'll change and be back, explore if you want, but that won't take long in this cracker-box size apartment."

"I'll be fine," she said. "Take your time."

He closed the door and she went into the kitchen and opened the oven and smelled the roast. Inside the refrigerator, she found a tossed salad and fresh strawberries.

When he came out, dressed in cutoffs with a white knit shirt, her eyes fixed on him. She felt the same excitement he generated when she first saw him. That feeling continued now, though more intense.

He had a white shirt in his hand. "This is the best I can offer."

He tossed it to her. He hurried by and opened the oven and picked up two potholders and lifted the pan out and placed it on the stove. He asked, "Broccoli, peas, or green beans? I have potatoes and carrots in with the roast."

"I like all three, you choose. May I use your bedroom to change?"

"Of course," he said.

He was opening a package of broccoli. She went into the bedroom and closed the door. The neat bed caught her eye. Instead of concern, she felt a shiver of excitement race down her spine. She slipped her dress over her head and pulled the shirt on and buttoned it to the top. It reached almost to her knees. She went to the bathroom and examined her face in the mirror. The shirt covered her body enough for modesty sake, but looking at herself, she decided the shirt was more seductive than her dress.

Sarah said to her image, "If he brought you here for sex, then the dress or this shirt won't make a difference." She lifted the shirt and examined her body and lingerie. Smiling, she dropped the shirt and went back to other room, her shoulders back, her head held high; ready for whatever Gary had planned.

She knew he had started the meal before earlier anticipating she would accept his invitation for lunch. She could have refused when she saw he brought her to his apartment, but since she met him, he hadn't made any attempts at anything sexual, except dancing close. She giggled silently, if this was his method of seduction, it was working.

He stood at the stove stirring gravy. When he saw her, he dropped the spoon.

Sarah laughed. "Did I scare you?"

"Hell yes, you scare the hell out of me. You're the most beautiful woman I've ever known."

She preened for him, holding the shirt, pressing it against her breast. "In this long baggy shirt?"

He found a long fork and fished for his spoon. "Can you do CPR?" he said as he pulled the spoon from the gravy.

"Why?" she giggled. "Do you have a heart problem?"

"I do now, seeing you made it miss a few beats."

She ignored his comment. "What can I do to help? Without the dress, I'm ready to contribute."

"Check the broccoli in the microwave, then set the table. The bread's about ready. I have tea if you'll fill the glasses with ice."

In the small kitchen, she had to move by him. She put her hand on his back and slit it across as she went by. His shoulder and back muscles bunched at her touch. Sarah loved the effect she had on him and marveled at the almost forgotten feeling of excitement with a man. She was comfortable with him. With Harold, there had been no intimate caressing or touching in ages. They were two people sharing the same house, but never having physical contact

27

and rarely speaking. They passed each other in the hall and never spoke.

She found the broccoli tender, and then located glasses in the cabinet and filled two with ice. He was putting bowels on the table when she placed two plates and silverware on the table.

He came to the bar with the roast. "If you'll have a seat, I'll finish," he said. "I'm starved; I've had nothing to eat since the picnic."

She sat and watched him work efficiently placing the food on the table. He filled her glass with tea and sat beside her. His hand moved over and covered hers as he said a short prayer. Never in her life had Sarah felt this sensation or as good. She was seated at a table, about to eat lunch with Gary, in his apartment, wearing his shirt, comfortable, contented, and glowing inside.

He passed her the platter of roast he had cut in thin slices. She took two, hungry for the meal he prepared for them. After they filled their plates, he paused and searched for her eyes. "May I say this?" he said without waiting for her consent. "If I read your face correctly, you're enjoying this as much as me. I learned to cook by necessity. If I wanted to eat anything besides frozen dinners, I had to learn."

She wanted to ask more, but held it in check.

"When Connie and I first married, she attempted to cook, a total disaster. Her heart wasn't in it. She fooled me. I can say I was young as the reason, but that's no excuse. But enough of that. I loved cooking for us. Eating alone and being alone is awful."

She held her fork between her plate and mouth, listening to him. She finished putting the bite in her mouth.

"Me saying I can cook doesn't mean a thing," she said. If you had told me you were an accomplished chef, I would have reserved judgment until I tasted your cooking. What I'm leading toward, I want to show you my culinary skills instead of telling you I'm a darn good cook. However, the opportunity to do that doesn't seem to be in the near future."

He put a bite in his mouth and chewed. "Maybe not as

long as you're thinking."

She waited, hoping he would add something to his statement. He didn't.

They chatted until they finished the meal. He brought a bowl of fresh strawberries covered with real whipped cream. She tasted the fresh fruit and smiled. His eyes met hers and bore deep into her.

"Mr. Justice," she managed, "a wonderful meal, everything was delicious. Since you cooked, I clean, but you sit there and coach me."

He leaned back and stretched his legs out from the bar. "Seems fair to me."

She laughed and jumped from her chair and began putting the dishes in the sink. He watched her legs under the shirt, lean and trim, agile.

"The bowls for the food are in the bottom drawer in the cabinet beside the stove."

She bent over to select the size she needed. He moaned as the shirt slid up her back. She rinsed the dishes and put them in the dishwasher, and then brought a towel to wipe the bar. She ignored him as she leaned across in front of him to reach the far side, and then tossed the towel back on the cabinet.

He stood and offered his hand and led her to the den and stopped in front of the couch. They sat side by side. Still holding her hand, he leaned back, pulling her close and put his arm around her. She settled beside him, her head on his shoulder. His lips played around her ears and cheek, and then she turned for their first kiss. It lasted for only a few seconds, but she shivered, not from cold, but from excitation. Gary's lips quivered as they meshed with hers again for a short, but meaningful kiss.

Neither spoke for a few minutes, and then he shifted where he could see her face. "Sarah, we, or I should say, I'm faced with a dilemma."

Her muscles tensed, anticipation, and then fear surged through her. Hoping he had the same feeling and will say it. His eyes searched for hers.

She sensed his predicament, feeling the same. "I need

to know, tell me," she said. With gentle fingers, she touched his sincere face, and then brushed his lips with hers. "I suggest we say what we feel, no holding back, completely honest. We get the facts out, and then we discuss them. I have the distinct feeling we have the same dilemma."

He gave her a subdued smile as he nodded agreement.

"Who goes first?" she asked.

"Since I started it," he said. "It's only fair I go first."

He took a deep breath. "Here goes. Going back to the picnic as the best place to start. I was waiting for you. I watched you and Harold come in and was stunned at your beauty. Then when our eyes met, the speech I had mentally prepared for you disappeared. You know the rest. Unplanned, it happened."

She waited, but he didn't follow through. "What happened?"

"By the time I left you last night, I was, I don't know how to put this in words, but I'll do my best. A deep feeling for you had developed. I wanted to be with you. When I got home, I had to hear your voice. The opportunity to be with you at church presented itself. Hoping you would accept the lunch invitation, I put the roast on to cook. You seated beside me, wearing my shirt, doing fantastic things with it, I guess, one way to say it, I've been searching for you. I've been looking for you for a long time."

Her emotions were on the verge of erupting. Her heart was beating a fast cadence on her ribs, her body heat becoming almost unbearable. She clamped her knees together, but her nipples were acting on their own, erect and sensitive against her bra and his shirt.

His arms circled her and she willingly turned and lay against his chest. She swallowed twice, hoping to relieve the dryness in her mouth. She faltered with her first attempt to speak. A little above a whisper, she said, "I'm married, but you're well aware of this. Harold is my husband on paper only. The marriage ended three years ago. I debated leaving him, but didn't. I read that alcoholism is a disease, a sickness. I stayed, hoping he would seek medical help. If alcoholism is a disease, why does he refuse medical attention? Why won't he seek help?"

She paused, and then clutched his hands he put them on her stomach. "We never have any intimacy." She turned her head more to see his face. "We agreed to be honest. So here it is. It's been almost three years since we tried to have sex and that was a disaster. He was drunk and abused me. He blamed me because he couldn't get an erection. He said I had no passion and a rubber doll would be better than having sex with me."

"But, now back to the present. When our eyes met at the picnic, you went deep into me. I couldn't pull away. But, I didn't want to pull my eyes from yours. I should have wanted to turn away, but I didn't. Then the man forced you to look at him to speak, I shifted my eyes away, but kept you in sight. I didn't have a clue who you were. I did know you made my pulse race. Then you came to me. As you said, you know the rest. When you asked me about church, I jumped at the chance to see you. I wanted to be with you for lunch. I want to be here with you now. I love being in your arms. You said you've been searching for me, here I am. You found me. Now what do we do?"

She wigged closer to him. "That brings us to now. Any suggestions?"

His fingers moved up and pressed under her breast. She held her breath, hoping he would continue, but he didn't.

She felt his need for her, hard and pressing against her thigh.

His arms tightened slightly. "I want you like I've never wanted a woman before. Not only for sex. I want you, like now, here with me. I want you where I can see you, close to me; where I can touch you, feel your body pressed against me. I want to hear your voice, your laugh, even hear you cry. Which I expect I will in the days to come. It could be tough."

"I've examined my mental state since meeting you," she said. "There's no guilt, my conscious is clear. So far we've only been together as friends. We kissed, but you haven't made a sexual gesture, except pressing under my breast, but that doesn't count. I feel your erection, but then, I felt that on the dance floor. I willingly put your shirt on, but then, I would have worn anything you gave me."

His fingers moved up and began unbuttoning the shirt. She put her hands on the back of his. He stopped.

"Gary, please understand. I want to go on, but not now. We only met yesterday. Please go slow with me. I'm married, even if it is to alcoholic. Our marriage ended a long while ago, but on paper, I'm still a married woman."

"I respect you for that Sarah. But it doesn't change what I'm feeling for you. I want to continue seeing you. When the time is right, well, we'll enjoy sex, but that isn't primary now. Being with you is much more important."

As if by something magic, their mouths met for a kiss. She felt a quiver cascade down his back and his muscles tensed. She knew he felt the same as her.

Sarah pulled her mouth from his so she could talk.

"Gary, I admit, I want to continue, there is no doubt of that, but not today. I'm grateful for what you have and are doing for me, but please understand."

His hands moved away from her back and she pushed back and stood.

"You're right," he said. "I apologize for my actions. I admit I want you so much I lost touch with reality. The attraction I have for you jammed my good judgment. Please forgive me."

"Forgiveness is not necessary. I willingly encouraged you. I came to your apartment and I'm wearing your shirt. I apologize for teasing you when I knew better. You make me feel all giddy inside and I'm not thinking rational. I have never been a passionate woman, but with you, well, I fully expect that will change. I have read and heard the most important sex organ is the brain. I never wanted sex with Harold, but with you, well." She let her voice trail off knowing she really didn't know what she wanted with him, except she wanted to be with him, in his arms.

Her cell phone rang. She cursed under her breath. "It has to be Harold. Should I answer?"

"No," then he said, "Yes, answer it. It may be for the best."

"Hello," she said. A string of curse words greeted her. Gary heard Harold and clutched her hand as he whispered in her ear. "You don't have to listen to that abuse."

He reached for the phone, but she held it away from him. "It's nothing new; he'll wind down in a minute and demand to know where I am. Shall I tell him I'm in his boss's apartment wearing one of his shirts?"

Gary almost grinned.

"I was teasing. I'll handle him."

When she could break in, she said, "Harold, stop it this instant. It's Sunday in case you forgot. I had lunch. I didn't expect you to be up this early, it's only two o'clock. After the binge at the picnic, I didn't expect you to wake until late this afternoon. You were in a drunken stumper, passed out on the picnic table. Mr. Justice and a young man named Marvin carried you to our car and then followed and put you on the bed."

He calmed, instantly and was silent for a few moments. "Did you say, Mr. Justice, Gary Justice?"

"Yes, the owner of the bank. You really made points with him."

He moaned. "I don't remember a thing. I guess I had one too many."

"One too many," she jabbed. "You had a dozen too many. You were out of it before they started serving dinner. I was so embarrassed; everybody saw you passed out at the picnic table."

"You should have helped me get in the car," he yelled.

"I couldn't lift you. You were unconscious, limp as a rag. It took booth Mr. Justice and Marvin to lift you and drag you to the car and into our house."

"It's your fault," he shouted. "Badgering me not to drink so much. If you had kept your mouth shut, I wouldn't have had so many."

She wanted to laugh at h is lame excuse, but held back. "Take responsibility for your actions instead of constantly blaming others for your drinking. You headed for the beer wagon almost in a run with your tongue hanging out. What I said or didn't say had no bearing. You need medical help."

He hung up.

Sarah shifted and placed both hands on Gary's cheeks. "I had better go. After that call, the mood we were in is gone. You know where I'll be if you want to call or see me."

She stood and started to walk toward the bedroom. He caught her hand and turned her to face him. His lips covered hers for their best kiss, ever. It was deep and good. She tasted him, his hard chest pressed against her naked breast. Her arms circled his neck and she kissed him with a need she never experienced before.

The kiss lasted until he had to hold her erect. Her body turned to soap suds, but his strong arms circled her and gave her support. On wobbly legs, she stood facing him.

His face flushed, his nostrils flared. She saw his desire and appreciation for her in his eyes.

He lifted her into his arms and carried her to the bedroom. He put her feet on the floor and looked at the bed with a wistful expression.

"Not now," he said. "It's not the right time yet."

She nodded, not sure, she understood until he glanced toward the bed again.

"This isn't a fling," he said. "We have time. It has to be right. I want to remember our first together with no blemishes."

"I understand and appreciate it," she whispered.

He watched her walk to the closet for her dress. She turned her back to him and removed his shirt and pulled the dress over her head and turned for him to close the zipper.

"Will you be okay with Harold?" he asked.

"Don't worry about me. By the time I get home, he'll be in the den with a quart of beer. In an hour, he'll be back in bed or on the floor. After he starts on one of his benders, it won't take all that much. I know he hasn't eaten, he never does when he's drinking."

"I still worry about you," he said. "After I found you, I don't want to lose you."

"You won't lose me," she said. "Call, that is, if you want."

"I have a better idea," he said. "When you can talk

34

freely, call me. You have this number."

"Are you sure?" she asked.

"Yes, I'm sure. Please call."

Chapter 3

As she expected, Harold was in the den with a quart of beer, almost empty. When he saw her, he yelled, "Where did you hide my car keys?"

"Where you can't find them," she slashed. "You can't drive in your condition. You would kill yourself or worse, kill somebody else."

He started toward with his fist swinging wildly. Sarah evaded him by stepping to the side and Harold went to the floor. He was cursing as loud as he could shout. He managed to get to his feet and stumbled toward her, again attempting to hit her. She backed away and pulled a chair in front of him.

He fell over it and lay on the floor glaring and cursing.

"Give me my keys," he demanded.

"No, keys, I'll get you beer. You may as well finish the job, drink yourself back into alcohol unconsciousness. Do you want a fifth of whisky so it'll work faster? I've seen liquor bottles you hid in the trash. I know you've reached the stage of drinking whisky and chasing it with beer."

"Make it a liter," he grumbled. "I have a feeling I'll need it tomorrow. I expect that young Justice will can me for something that wasn't my fault. They have it in for me at the bank."

She turned and walked out the door and drove to the liquor store. Sarah returned with the booze, she took him a quart of beer and a liter of the cheapest whisky she could buy. The quart beer bottle he had been drinking, now empty, was on the floor. She put the full bottles on the table beside his chair and faced him. "Do I wake you to go to work tomorrow?"

He rolled his head back and swallowed. "I may as well go in and get it over with."

36

"Do you need help getting to the bed?" she asked. "If you pass out here, you stay here. I won't carry you to bed."

He mumbled as he swallowed another mouth full of whisky and chased it with a generous amount of beer.

"Harold, don't ever try to hit me again."

"Screw you," he said. "Don't hide my keys again."

She left and went to her bedroom and lay on the bed and reached for the phone. Gary answered on the first ring. "Hi, it's me," she said.

"Is everything okay there?" he asked with obvious concern in his voice.

"I'm fine. He was already drinking again. A quart of beer was almost empty and he was mad because I hid his keys. He tried to hit me because I hid his car keys. He was too drunk get close enough and fell to the floor I went for more booze, in about ten minutes he'll be passed out in the den. I told him to get in the bed because I can't lift him."

"I told him to never attempt to hit me again. He said, screw you. That was the first time he has been violent and tried to hurt me. He is getting worse. He scared me."

Gary moaned. "In that case, come back to me. You can go to work from here tomorrow morning."

She paused, considering his request, knowing what to expect if she went back to him. A thrill shot through her like a hot poker before settling in her loins. "I can't do that. Remember, we haven't reached that stage as yet."

"Then can we talk on the phone for a few minutes?" he asked.

"What do you want to discuss?" she asked.

"Us," he said.

She clutched the other pillow to her breast wishing for him. She felt his happiness even though they were talking on the phone. "Us?" she said.

"Where we go from here, together," he said.

"Yes sir," she said as she sighed in contentment.

"You're married to an alcoholic and he has reached the violent stage. This presents a problem, it's going to get worse as he's going to be unemployed shortly. He may twist off completely."

"I know, but I fear your meeting with him won't be tomorrow. I doubt he'll be able to function for a couple of days. There was still booze and he won't stop until it's gone. He'll demand I go for more if this binge hasn't run its course."

"Whether it's tomorrow or the next day, even the later part of the week, the results will be the same. That leads to what we do."

"What do you want me to do?" she asked.

"How do we deal with Harold," he said.

"What do you mean by that?" she asked.

"Do you agree it has ended between you and Harold? I mean your marriage," he said.

She didn't consider his question for more than a second before she replied. "It's over. That stunt he pulled at the picnic was the last straw. I intend to file for divorce."

"I agree with that decision. It's time to divorce him and move on with your life."

"Just like that, file for divorce and move on," she said.

"Yes," he replied.

"May I ask a couple of questions?"

"Of course, ask," he said.

"We only met. You don't know me. I don't know you. What we have may be infatuation, loneliness, or pure lust. I suggest we see each other for a while. That is, if you want to see me. We should give it time; see if we're compatible. See if we mesh for more than the moment. A short-term fling or one nightstand is not what I want."

"What you say about giving it time has merit. Sarah, I want you with me. I know this is where you belong, with me. It's not due to loneliness, even though I'm lonesome living alone. It's more than infatuation, that phase passed when I was a teen. Lust, maybe, I want you, I can't or won't deny that, but I assure you, I want more than sex. A lot more."

"I believe you, until proven wrong," she said. "If we use our head, we can see each other. I want more time with you, to get to know about you. Harold will never know. Booze is all he thinks or cares about now. I never see him after dinner. He goes to the den with his bottles, that is, if he doesn't eat there, which is most of the time now. He usually starts drinking before he gets home and never lets up."

Gary grunted in disgust at Harold's actions. "I'll agree to that. we see each other every evening. If we are still comfortable and want to continue, on the twenty-first, that's on a Friday. Will you go to the ranch with me for the weekend? We can come back Tuesday after Memorial Day."

"I want to do that," she said. "But please don't push me into doing something we'll regret. I truly want to be with you, but what about Harold?"

"Between now and the twenty-first, we work on having him volunteer to enter an abuse institution. For him and both our sakes, that would be best."

"I know," she said between clinched teeth. "It's what he needs. If he agrees, if he gets control of his problem, what then?"

"As I said earlier, divorce him. You said it's over. Your marriage is on paper only."

"That's true," she said, "But, if I divorce him, it's possible Harold would never recover. I'm also concerned what he will do when I tell him I want a divorce. Harold is very jealous and possessive. He may turn more violent. I mean do more than try to hit me when he is drinking."

"The only way to find out is tell him. Do you love him?" he asked. "Do you have feelings for him?"

"I can honestly say I don't love him. Of that I'm positive. Any love I had died a long time ago. Feelings, yes. I feel sorry for him and pity him. I want to help him, but at the same time, my feelings, and in my heart, I know I want to be with you. Her thoughts ranged farther, to be Gary's wife and the mother of his children.

As if he knew what she was thinking, he said, "The have a positive feeling that the time is within the foreseeable future when we'll marry and I want us to have children."

A surge of excitement rushed through her body. He read her mind. "You want me to have your baby?" she asked as she clutched the pillow.

"More than anything in this world. When the time is right, you'll be my wife, and we'll offer the world another

39

Justice to carry on the tradition."

At that moment, hearing his words, she knew without a doubt, she was absolutely and completely in love with Gary Justice. The thought of his baby in her womb was more than she could handle, an uncontrollable paroxysm sparked through her. Her body shook in almost spasms and her breath became ragged.

"What happened to you?" he asked. "I felt or heard something, even over the phone. Something surged through your body like electricity."

She barely managed as she gasped for air. "I fell in love with you, totally and completely. The thought of being your wife and our baby in my body overruled every concern."

He gave a whoop of excitement. "God woman, I love you. I've known since yesterday, but waited to say it."

Their emotions were an all time high, each savoring their intimacy.

"Goodnight, darling," she whispered.

"Wait a second before you hang up," he said. "I'll call you at your break."

"I'll be in my room so we can talk freely."

"You don't think Harold will wake and come to work?" he asked.

"I seriously doubt it. He'll continue on his binge until the booze is gone. It would do no good to wake him, as he couldn't function anyway. He's in a stupor and he'll sleep until noon, or later."

Chapter 4

Sarah's drive to the school was filled with thoughts, replaying her time with Gary, and relishing her newly discovered emotional state. Being a woman again filled her with a warm glow. Having a man like Gary was more than she ever dreamed. He took her higher than she thought possible, and she wanted more of what only he could offer.

Her entire body tingled with a delight she hadn't experienced in years, if ever. It had taken an extra application of makeup to cover his whisker burns, but it was worth it to feel in kiss. Gary had raised her vitalities for life to an unbelievable level, and she relished the prospect of a future, with him.

Her best friend, Abby, greeted her with a smile. Her first words startled Sarah. "What happened to you? You look great. I've never seen you glowing like today. I expected you to drag in looking awful. I heard about Harold at the picnic. Beth from the bank told me he drank himself into oblivion and Gary Justice and Marvin helped you put him in the car. She said he was in a stupor, limp as a rag."

Sarah nodded.

Abby pushed for more information. "Then what happened to you? After that much to drink, Harold had to be a total A.H." Abby always used acronyms for what she considered dirty words.

"Nothing much," Sarah replied. She wasn't about to tell Abby about Gary. That bit of gossip would spread like wildfire.

"Don't give me that B S," Abby demanded. "Something happened." Abby tapped her forehead in thought. "Of course, that hunk, Gary Justice, wonderful. Chunk that worthless Harold in the dumpster, and go for it. I understand he owns a ranch as well as the bank. Beth said you danced with him the entire night."

Sarah hated to lie to her friend, but saw no choice. With Abby's wagging tongue, it would be all over school in a matter of hours. She would confide with her other friends and the news of Sarah and Gary would burst into the gossip mill to be circulated and embellished to the point of Sarah and Gary having a torrent love affair. She inwardly smiled, which could easily happen. "I'm sorry to pop your balloon. Mr. Justice and Marvin helped me load Harold in the car. When I got home, they put Harold on the bed and left. I let him sleep. He woke and drank himself back into a state of unconsciousness. When I left this morning, he was on the floor in the den, passed out."

Abby didn't give up. "Something happened. A disgusting weekend with that drunk didn't make you look like Miss Sunshine walking on rose pedals this morning."

Suddenly Abby blurted out with an answer. "You got laid. Who was he, Justice?"

"I have no idea what you're talking about. I did make a decision and feel better now. That may be it. I do have a heavy weight off my shoulders. I decided I'm not going to let Harold drag me down anymore. I've had enough. That stunt he pulled at the picnic was the final straw. He won't admit he has a problem and refuses to discuss treatment. School will soon be out and by fall, things will have changed, drastically. I decided to file for divorce and move on with my life." Again the truth, just not the whole story.

Abby's eyes went to Sarah's face. "You finally intend to divorce that worthless bum? A few years overdue, but late is better than never."

"What Harold needs is to be committed to an abuse institution," Abby said.

"He won't agree to that," Sarah said. "He rants and raves that he doesn't have a problem. It has gotten to the point his anger scares me."

Abby played another card in her arsenal. "Beth told me the rumor around the bank is that Justice is going to fire Harold. How do you feel about that? Will that be a wedge between you and Gary?"

"A wedge? How can that be since I barely know the man? I met him on Saturday and we danced. To be honest, I think Mr. Justice felt sorry for me. I was seated alone at a picnic table and he came to me to talk about Harold. In fact, I wouldn't blame Mr. Justice if he fired Harold. I know Harold can't perform in his current condition." Again, she didn't lie, just evaded the whole truth.

Abby gave up. "I'll keep this between us."

"Keep what between us. What Harold did at the picnic is already common knowledge, too many people saw what happened. Gary and I danced at the picnic with a several other couples. When I file for a divorce, everybody in town will know."

Knowing Abby is incapable of keeping a secret, she hoped this would satisfy her. If there were no dirt to gossip about, hopefully, she would go off in another direction and find some other spicy topic.

Sarah skipped lunch and took care of the financial business Gary recommended. She opened a bank account at another bank and filed the necessary forms to have her salary deposited in the new account.

At her break, she sat at her desk, her cell phone in front of her. The ringing made her jump, even though she expected Gary to call.

"Hello beautiful," he said. "I love you."

"Hi handsome, and I love you. How has your day been?"

"Never better. I had several people ask why I was feeling so chipper. I told them a beautiful woman."

"Please tell me you didn't give them my name. Abby, my best friend asked me the same question. She said I was glowing and called me Miss Sunshine. She even asked who laid me. I hopefully convinced her that my cheerful appearance was because I made the decision about my life and things are going to improve drastically. I told her I was going to file for a divorce."

"That's all true," he said.

"I'm not going back to the place I was, for the good or bad. I'm moving on with my life."

"With me," he said. From his tone, she knew it was not a question, but a statement of fact. He truly felt her place was with him.

"More than likely. I can't think of not being with you."

"Me neither. I need you. But now, to the more serious matter, Harold didn't show as you predicted."

"I expected as much. Do you want me to call him?"

"I'll leave that up to you. You know a lot more than me how to handle him."

"He's going to be horrible when he sobers up and mad as a hornet. I hid the car keys. Without walking, he can't buy more booze, and it's miles to the nearest liquor store."

"That is best for his sake and others on the streets. Did you open a new account?" he asked.

"I did as you recommended. I know that was a smart move on my part. I changed my salary so it would go there."

"Give me that information, and I'll make sure the money you have in this bank is transferred."

She gave him the information without hesitation.

"Can you meet me tonight?" he asked.

"What do you have in mind?" she asked.

"We'll go to dinner as soon as you can get away."

"Okay, it's a date," she said.

"You have my private number," he said. "Please call if anything happens. I need to know and please call me from your house as soon as you get there and check out the situation. I want to know you're safe."

Harold has never really hurt me. He has pushed, shoved, and slapped me. But, he mostly yells and screams, curses me, and blame me for everything, but he's never hit me with his fist. Well he never has, but then, I've never hid the keys, emptied the bank account, or cancelled our credit cards before."

"Be extra careful," Gary warned. "He's falling deeper and deeper and may lose his sense of reality." Then he paused and spoke softly with genuine sincerity. "I love you Sarah. And even though I want you so much I ache all the time, it's not just lust for your sexy body. I want you as my partner, my best friend, and someday, my wife and the

44

mother of our children."

Her heart pounded. "I love you," she said.

She touched the end button and sat looking at the phone. It rang, she wondered if Gary called again. She looked at the screen and saw it was Harold. She was right, he yelled the second she answered.

With the phone six inches from her ear, she waited for him to slow down. "Why didn't you wake me this morning," he demanded. "I'm going to be fired, and it's your fault."

She spoke, softly, but with meaning. "I'm through babysitting you. You're an out of control alcoholic and need professional help. You can get up either on your own, stay in bed, or on the floor. I don't give a damn anymore. After the stunt you pulled at the picnic, I'm through. I can't take it anymore."

"Where did you hide my car keys?" he demanded.

"I'm not telling you, sober up, eat something. You don't need any more alcohol."

"I called twice and the line was busy, who were you talking with?" he demanded.

"The bank, they asked where you were. I told them the last time I saw you, you were passed out on the den floor."

He moaned. "You're trying to get me fired."

"A lot of people say you have to hit bottom before you'll admit to being an alcoholic. Being fired appears to be what it'll take for you to admit you have a problem."

He hung up. She instantly called Gary. "Harold called, mad as hell. I told him he needs help. He hung up on me."

"What do you intend to do?" he asked

"Go home and see what state he's in and give him something to eat, but I doubt he'll eat. He'll demand I give him the keys, or demand I go for more booze. After he passes out in the den, I'll meet you."

"Perfect, wear a dress, cocktail. We're going out for dinner and dancing."

"We can't do that, this town is too small, and we would be seen. It would cause me trouble. With a divorce looming. You know what I'm saying."

"I have a place in mind. We won't be seen by anybody

45

we know. It's only a few miles from here, but we can enjoy the drive and you come down from the stress of the day."

She couldn't even think of saying, no. "What color do you like?"

"With you, white," he said.

Sarah smiled, wishing she had met Gary first, but then the past can't be changed. She knew her only option was go forward, making the best of the situation. And hopefully, that was pointing more and more toward Gary.

She paused in thought.

"What are you thinking about?" he asked. "If we should go out for dinner and dancing?"

"Yes and no, mostly, I was thinking about my future with you."

"It is, you know," he whispered with affection in his voice.

"I truly hope so. I'll rush to the house, and see the condition of Harold." She realized she used the word house, instead of home, and wondered why.

***

As soon as she could manage after the last bell of the day, she hurried to her car and drove home. She noticed a liquor store and made a spur of the moment decision. She stopped and bought a liter of cheap 100 proof whisky and four quarts of beer.

She knew he wouldn't stop drinking, and this would beat having a fight over the keys. He was going to demand more alcohol and she might as well take it now as giving to go back after it. As she told Gary, he would demand the keys, or demand she go for more liquor. She knew from experience, he would take money from her purse and forcibly take her car if she didn't supply him with liquor.

He was steaming for a fight when she walked in. His face red and both fist doubled into fist. "Where are my car keys?" he screamed.

"Hidden so you won't hurt somebody driving drunk. Take this and go back into your den and leave me alone. I'll make something for you to eat."

He grabbed the booze and turned and stumbled toward

46

the den. He was still under the influence.

She hurried to the kitchen, made a ham and cheese sandwich, put a handful of chips beside it, and took it to the den. Harold ignored her as she put it on a table near him.

He had the liquor open and was taking a swallow and chasing it with beer. Sarah noticed the liquor bottle was down by a third. She knew he wouldn't eat, but she tried. He looked at her with bleary eyes. The liquor was already taking effect on his partly pickled brain.

"Anything else?" she asked. "I have a meeting." Sarah desperately wanted to say, a date with Gary. Instead, she said, "I may be late. We're going out to eat afterwards, celebrating the end of school." This was partly true.

He nodded and took a long healthy swallow of whisky and guzzled beer.

"Tomorrow morning," she said in disgust. "I'm not waking you."

"Screw you," he shouted.

She called Gary as she promised. "Everything is under control. I'll be leaving as soon as I shower and dress."

He sighed, partly from relief that she was okay, and she was coming to him. "Please hurry, I need to hold you and kiss your sweet lips."

"I'll be there as soon as I can. Ready for both."

She went to her bedroom and selected lingerie and the white cocktail dress she would wear and hurried to the bathroom for a quick shower. She dressed and went to the den. Harold was laying in the recliner, the whisky in one hand, and the beer in the other. A game was on T V.

She walked in front of him and put her hands on her hips in disgust. "I'm going now."

He didn't reply; he was already out of it for the night. She noticed the sandwich, untouched.

Chapter 5

She drove toward Gary's apartment, frowning at her situation. Being forced to have an affair, but wanting to be with Gary. She desperately needed his arms around her and his lips on hers.

He met her with concern etched on his face. He noticed the expression on her face. "Is everything under control?" he asked.

"I'll tell you about it when we're inside." He reached for her hand and they went inside the apartment. Gary again looked at her face and expression and opened his arms for her. She welcomed his embrace and pressed close. "Hold me," she said, softly, clutching him with her arms. "Is what I'm doing the right thing?"

"Absolutely," he said with assurance. "We belong together."

"I hope so, but let me tell you what I did."

He lifted her into his arms and carried her to the couch and sat beside her. His arms circled her and he kissed her lips, softly, with love.

"Now tell me," he said.

She pushed back to see his face. "I wanted to be with you, and I knew a way where it would be safe. I stopped and bought him a supply of booze. He was furious when I got home, shouting about the keys. But when he saw the bottles, he took them and went to the den. I made him a sandwich."

She saw a small smile on his face and felt better. She added, telling him everything. "I told him I had a meeting, rather than a date with you. I told him I would be late. He ignored me. Then I told him that tomorrow morning I wasn't going to wake him. He said screw you, again."

He hugged her and held her tight. She relished his understanding and concern.

48

"You don't think I'm a bitch for doing that to Harold?"

His face turned hard and he gripped his jaws so tight she saw the tendons in his neck extend. He held her with steel fingers, not hurting her, but firmly. "Never use that word in front of me, referring to yourself."

She gasped, hearing his tone of voice. "I won't ever again, I promise," she managed.

"You're a lady of the highest respect I've ever met." He bore into her. You are my wife to be and the mother or our children. The word bitch or slut will never be used when talking about yourself, is that understood?"

"Yes sir," she whimpered.

He softened and his grip, which turned into a gentle caress. "Harold would have gotten booze, one way of the other, either forcing you to give him the keys, or making you drive for him or sending you after it. This way, he's off the street. You did right, the only way, the best way. He'll never stop without treatment. He's so hooked, he doesn't want to stop and you or I can't make him. He has to want to quit."

Sarah felt better.

"One other thing," he said. "I want to tell you while we're discussing this. We'll never screw or fuck."

Surprise flashed on her face, wondering what he meant.

"We'll make sweet love, only that. Sex between will be a part of loving. Never use the F word when discussing our relationship."

Her heart wanted to burst with love for him. He was so different from Harold; he used the F word back when he was able to perform. If he ever said, make love, she didn't remember it. She kissed him with love on her lips. "I understand the difference. Harold never made love to me, he F'd me."

He stood, still holding her in his arms. "Enough of the melancholy, from this point forward, only fun and happy things. We have reservations for dinner and dancing, and I love the dress. I need my coat and we'll be on the way."

Her mood changed dramatically at his words. Happily, she teased his lips with hers.

***

Sarah felt like a teen on her first date. She sat beside him, her head on his shoulder, and his arm around her when he could while driving. He drove into the country and stopped in front of a hotel located beside a lake. Flowers of many colors decorated the driveway and she saw gentle sloping grass that led to the blue water of the lake. "We may spend a night or two on our honeymoon," he said. "Should we marry here in the city, I know I won't drive far."

She kissed his cheek, but didn't ask why. She knew what he meant.

He had reservations for a table on the deck overlooking the lake. A three person combo was playing dinner music as they dined. A bottle of delicious wine was in a silver bucket beside their table.

He poured her wine and they talked until the bottle was almost empty before he requested another and they ordered the meal. As with the wine, the meal was outstanding. They enjoyed fresh strawberries and whipped cream for dessert. Sarah had never been treated in such a wonderful manner and she loved the attention and thoughtfulness.

He stood and offered his hand and led her out on the floor. They danced as one, her arms around his neck, with his right hand on the small of her back and the other high up just under her neck. His fingers caressed the bare skin on her back and his lips teased her ears. She welcomed him with her lips on his neck as he pressed her close.

Her body fused to him as they swayed to the music with his thighs between hers. On a dreamy love song, she felt his need for her. In perfect rhythm, she responded, holding him close. Near the end of the song, she couldn't hold back and a small climax surged.

He felt it and kissed her waiting lips.

When she relaxed, his arms supported her weakened body. "That was the most beautiful thing I've ever seen or felt," he whispered into her ear. Her lips covered his and she wanted to attach her body to him, permanently.

When the song ended, on rickety legs, he led her to their table.

50

"This is the way a man and woman in love should be together," he said.

She welcomed his touch on her cheeks and neck as he leaned forward. "It's been wonderful, and this is the first of many times we'll enjoy dinner and dancing, but we both have to work tomorrow. Are you ready to go?"

"No, but I know you're right. Maybe on a Friday or Saturday night we can stay until the band kicks us out."

"It's a date," he said.

She sat close, her head on his shoulder as he drove. He stopped beside her car and pulled her close for a goodnight kiss. "Someday soon, I'll carry you inside," he said.

She expected he was right and wondered if she could or would object if he did it tonight.

***

Gary called during her break. "I love you," he said immediately upon hearing her voice.

"And I love you," she sighed.

"Howard didn't report for work again."

"I'm not surprised, as we've discussed, if he has booze, he won't stop drinking. He was passed out in the recliner when I got there last night, and was still in the chair when I left for work this morning."

"Are you going to your house before coming tonight?" he asked.

"I don't know, should I? I mean, if I go there, do I take more booze?"

"We can postpone the confrontation a few more days, and then let him fend for himself for a change."

"Is that smart? I mean, he may go ballistic and do something awful."

"A thought," he said. "We maintain the status quo until Wednesday before school is out on Friday. He sobers up and comes to the bank on Friday. I give him the ultimatum, treatment or else."

"Are saying I should take him more booze today?"

"Only if you think it best, for you, for him, for us."

She stopped and bought a liter of the cheap bourbon. Quality wasn't what Harold wanted; he wants volume. A case of quart bottles of beer and four liters of whisky should keep him supplied for a few more days she thought.

He was in the den when she entered the house, waiting for her. She noticed the sandwich was gone and saw the plate on the floor. Empty bottles were scattered around the room. She put the alcohol on the table and walked in front of him. He looked at her, not fully focusing.

"Want something to eat or more booze?"

"Hand me the whisky and beer," he said.

Sarah handed him a bottle of liquor and a quart of beer. "Did you eat the sandwich?" she asked.

"I think so. I was supposed to go to work today."

"I know," she said with contempt in her voice.

Sarah turned and went to the kitchen and made him another sandwich and put it on the table beside him, and bent over for the empty plate and carried it back to the sink. She left the empty bottles on the floor.

She went to her bedroom to change. She would soon be in Gary's arms. Harold was still seated in the recliner with a bottle in either hand. "How long are you going to stay drunk?" she asked.

He looked up with blurry eyes. She could tell he didn't comprehend her question. "I'm leaving," she said. She didn't bother to give an excuse. He was beyond understanding anyway.

He grunted and pulled on the whisky, she saw him swallow three times and a bubble went up the bottle. He put it down and guzzled beer, and then belched loudly before he mumbled something as she walked away and went out the front door.

Gary again waited when she stopped in front of his apartment. She walked at his side and stopped inside the door. He closed it and pulled her into his arms for an affectionate hug. "I'm glad to see you," he said.

She didn't respond to him today.

He saw her face and concern flooded his eyes and expression.

Sarah met his gaze. "I feel guilty. I took him more booze and he was already so out of it he couldn't understand what I said."

He folded her into his arms and put her head against his chest. His understanding fingers stroked her hair and cheeks. "Before I left Harold, I told him I was leaving. He didn't have a clue what I said."

He let her talk, realizing she needed to get it out so they could deal with it, together.

"He ate the sandwich I made him last night, so I made another and left it on the table. I can't help it. I love you and want to be here, but I worry if what I did was the right thing. That's twice I've done that to be with you."

He lifted her into his arms and carried her to the couch, sat down, and pulled her back against his chest. His strong arms circled her and his lips kissed her hair and cheeks.

"Sarah," he spoke softly with love in his voice. "Please understand; you can't help him. I can't help him. He's the only one, and he refuses to let professionals administer the treatment he must have to turn his life around. In Harold's case, I would say the odds of that happening are very small. Unfortunately, not every alcoholic or addict can be saved. Just like every cancer patient can't be cured."

She turned in his arms. "I understand, but tonight, I feel guilty for some reason. I've tried so many times, but he refuses to even discuss it."

"When did you eat?" he asked, effectively changing the subject, for her sake.

"I had half of a sandwich for lunch. I wasn't hungry. I'm not hungry now, except for you. This is what I need, your arms around me."

He kissed her lips lightly and held her in his arms until he felt her relax, somewhat.

"Will you go with me to the kitchen and see what we can find. I skipped lunch and I'm starved."

She jumped from the couch and reached for his hand. "I'm sorry, I was selfish, I was only thinking of myself."

"Nonsense, but I do need one of your beautiful smiles."

Sarah smiled, not a huge one, but better than the frown, she had been wearing.

"Look into my eyes," he said.

53

Again, he bore deep into her core as only he could do. "I love you with all my heart," he said."

Her emotions overruled and her lips met his in a demanding, torrid kiss. She tasted blood as their teeth cut their lips and cheeks. She knew her mouth would be bruised, but she didn't care.

Her fury quickly passed and she pulled back to look at him.

Too her relief, she saw his love for her reflected in his eyes and on his face. His smile warmed her, his hands moved on her back, gentle and reassuring massaging from her neck to her buttocks. Their eyes linked and froze in place. "I'm sorry," she whispered.

"Sorry," he said in disbelief, he didn't understand. "I've never experienced anything so beautiful, so absolutely perfect. I want you to come to me when you're in the state you were in tonight, wanting me and needing me."

She kissed him and winced, it hurt her lips. She pulled back and sensed his discomfort as well. "I hurt you, didn't I? I kissed you so hard I tasted blood in my mouth."

"I wouldn't have had it any other way," he said.

She kissed him again, gentle this time, their lips savoring the other.

She reached for his hand. He saw a very different Sarah. Her eyes were bright and glowing; happiness was etched on her face.

"Now," she said. "It's time to feed my man."

The happy couple went to the kitchen. "Sit," she said. "I'll see what we have to eat."

She opened cabinets and saw the bourbon and turned to him. "Do you want a cocktail before dinner?"

He nodded, "That would be nice, with you."

She poured a healthy jigger into glasses and added ice. She walked to him and handed one to him and they touched glasses. "To Gary, my superman," she said.

They took a sip and they both winched at the burning sensation due to the cuts on their lips and cheeks.

She turned and searched the cabinets and refrigerator and found the roast he cooked for her and held it up for him

54

to see. "Perfect," he said. "A sandwich would hit the spot."

She sat at the bar with him as they ate. "I'm hungry now," she said with her mouth full. "Before, the thought of food never entered my mind."

They both ate every bite, and then she picked up their plates and took them to the sink and rinsed them before putting them in the dishwasher. She turned and he was waiting for her.

He lifted her into his arms and carried her to the couch. As usual, she lay back against him and enjoyed his arms around her. She shifted until she could see his face.

"I feel good now. When I got here tonight, I was almost a basket case. I've never needed anyone like I needed your support and understanding. I was so keyed up, I was about to explode inside."

He held her and they talked, keeping the conversation light and cheery. The time for depression had passed for her. The time flew by for them.

He paused a moment, and then gave her a hug and glanced at his watch. "I know it's only eleven o'clock, but we both have to work tomorrow."

"Someday, instead of me walking you to your car, I'll carry you to our bed."

"I wish we could do that tonight, but we must be strong and play this out," she said.

Chapter 6

Gary called at her break as usual. They greeted each other with the usual. "I love you."

"Harold didn't come in again," he said.

"He won't as long as he has alcohol. He was on the floor when I left this morning. I guess he slid out of the chair or fell. I checked him and he was okay, just passed out."

"Will I see you again tonight?" he asked.

"Of course, but may I buy food and cook a candlelight dinner for you. I think that will be more romantic than going out. I hate to say it, but your cabinet is bare as far as food is concerned."

"I would love that, our first meal you cook for us."

She dressed in jeans and a shirt and topped and bought a supply of things Gary needed. The meal was a success. He asked her to watch as he did the dishes, and then they went to the couch were she settled in her favorite place with her back against his chest and his arms around her.

***

For the next few days, Sarah managed to be with Gary every evening and as the time passed they felt more comfortable and relaxed together. On Wednesday night before the showdown with Harold on Friday, he outlined his plan to her.

"Let me go to your house tomorrow and confront Harold. I'll give him an ultimatum to either sober up, come to work, or he'll be dealt with, or without him being at the bank on Friday.

Not knowing the state Harold would be in; Gary bought a fifth of whisky and two quarts of beer. Not an abundant supply for an alcoholic because he wanted Harold to be sober for their meeting on Friday.

He stopped in the driveway and rang the bell several

times. "I'm coming, hold your horses," Harold growled.

When he opened the door, Gary almost gagged. Harold smelled awful. He had thrown up and soiled himself. He didn't recognize Gary. "What the hell do you want?" he snarled.

"I'm Gary Justice from the bank. You haven't reported for work in several days, and we were concerned."

"It's Sarah's fault," he grumbled. "She didn't wake me."

"I see. Can I come in?"

Harold stepped back and Gary went inside. He struggled to keep his voice at a controlled level, fighting back the urge to lash out at his employee. "Have you eaten anything?" he asked, forcing a concerned reflection in his question.

Harold looked confused as he considered the question. "I don't know."

Gary went to the den and saw an empty plate on the floor. "You must have, I see a plate on the floor beside your chair."

"Maybe I did, I don't remember."

"Friday, I want you to come to the bank. Sober up tomorrow and be at the bank on Friday morning."

"Why," Harold demanded. "You're going to fire me anyway. Do it now and I won't have to dress and face the embarrassment of being tossed out the front door on my ass."

"You're not going to be fired."

Harold looked confused, then stated. "Why not?" he said.

"I want us to have a talk. There are several issues we must discuss."

Gary looked around the den and saw the empty bottles. Without asking, he went to the kitchen and looked in the refrigerator and saw there was no alcohol.

"Do you have any left," Gary asked.

"I was going after more, but I can't find my keys. Sarah hid them from me."

Gary pointed toward the hallway. "Go into the bathroom and shower. I brought you enough to make it

57

through the night, but not enough for tomorrow. You must sober up."

Harold stated in amazement. "You brought me a drink?"

"You can have it, but not before you shower. Put on fresh clothes, you smell awful. Shave while you're there." It was obvious he hadn't since before the picnic.

He waited until Harold went into the bathroom and heard the water running, and then went to his car and brought in the bottles. He quickly made Harold a sandwich, and put it on the bar. Harold came back dressed in shorts and a shirt. He had shaved and used some kind of lotion. He smelled much better.

Gary pointed at the food. "Sit and eat before we talk."

Harold reached for the beer and put it on the table. Gary put his hand on the beer bottle. "Eat it all, or you don't get it."

He watched until Harold finished, then Harold grabbed the quart and downed over a third of it before he stopped for a breath of air. Gary put the fifth of liquor on the table. He hoped he had judged right on the quantity.

Harold picked up the liquor and beer and went to the den. He sat in the recliner and tired to focus on his watch. "What time is it?" he asked.

Gary glanced at his watch. "Almost three."

"Sarah will be here soon."

"I see," Gary said. She and Gary had agreed she would wait at his apartment to see how it went between Harold and Gary.

Harold removed the lid from the whisky and tossed it toward the trash, then turned the bottle up and swallowed several times.

Gary watched him chase it with beer. He knew Harold would never know if Sarah came home or not.

He pulled a chair close and sat across from Harold. "If you aren't at the bank by noon Friday, I'll call you."

Harold nodded, but didn't appear to hear or comprehend. At the moment, he didn't care. He had alcohol.

Gary left Harold seated in the recliner working on the booze. As soon as he could, he called his apartment. Sarah answered. "Hello," she said, timidly.

"May I speak with the lady of the house?" he said, trying to disguise his voice.

She recognized his voice immediately, and replied with glee. "Speaking."

"I'm leaving Harold. He's fine. He took a shower and I made him a sandwich. He ate it and has started on liquor and beer. I hope I gauged it right and he'll be out of booze in time to sober up tomorrow and report to the bank on Friday."

"Gary, are we doing the right thing? I know I've asked this before, but, well you know. Are we keeping him so inebriated he won't know I'm with you?"

"Just until tomorrow, it'll all change. He and I'll have our talk Friday and I'll lay it on the line to him. School will be out and we'll go to the ranch."

"When will you be home?" she asked.

"What did you say?"

"I asked when you'll be home."

He pretended not to hear again. "When will I be, where?"

She giggled. "You heard me the first time. Come home. I need to see my man, and I have cocktails ready to make and dinner in the oven."

"Give me thirty minutes," he said.

"I have comfortable clothes laid out for you."

"What do you have on?" he asked.

"The shirt, of course."

She met him at the door and stepped into his arms for a kiss, and then took his hand and led him to bedroom. He handed her his coat and worked on his shirt. She took the coat to the closet and caught the shirt he tossed to her. She carried it to the hamper while he removed his pants and stepped into the shorts and pulled a soft knit shirt over his wide shoulders. "Now, beautiful lady, what was that about a cocktail."

She again reached for his hand and led him to the

couch. "Sit here and I'll have it ready in a jiff."

Sarah hurried to the kitchen and came back and put two drinks on the side table and sat beside him. She handed him his drink and touched his glass with hers, they took a sip.

"What happen when you went to check on Harold?" she asked.

He relayed the incident in detail. "Hopefully, he'll be sober tomorrow and he and I can have our meeting."

She winched at his comment. "I have a big concern about him doing that. I hope he doesn't try to buy more instead of going to the bank."

"Me too, but this has to end sometime. If he doesn't show, I'll go to his house again."

She sighed as his arms circled her. They finished their drinks in silence and she stood. "I'll make you another while I put the food on the table. Relax until I call you."

He lay back, watching her, marveling at her agility, and the sureness of her movements.

A few minutes later, she came to him and reached for his hands and pulled. "It's ready." She led him to the table and sat across from him so she could see his face. She put a fillet minion on his plate and handed him a baked potato. A tossed salad was in a bowl in front of his plate. She uncovered a bowl of steamed broccoli and slices of Texas toast.

He looked at the food in front of him, then up at her smiling face. "Will you marry me?" he said.

"As they say, the way to man's heart is through his stomach," but she didn't answer his question. He noticed, but didn't comment. When the time was right, he would ask on bended knees.

They chatted trivia until he wiped the last of the juice from his plate with a piece of bread and leaned back. She went to the oven and brought him a slice of steaming hot chocolate pie, then hurried to the freezer for ice cream.

He used his spoon to scoop up the last crumb of pie from his bowl, and then looked at her. "I guess you know if you continue to cook like that, I'll need larger clothing, and you may be working yourself into a point we rarely go out to

60

eat."

"If I put weight on you, then I'll be forced to work it off," she giggled.

"And how will you do that, at a gym, walking in the evenings, or jogging every morning?"

"None of the above," she glanced at the bedroom with her eyes.

"Oh that," he chuckled.

She laughed with him. He stood and began taking the empty bowls and plates to the kitchen. She helped him and rinsed the dishes and put them in the dishwasher.

Her mind flashed to Harold, he never went into the kitchen, except for beer.

He lifted her into his arms and took her to the couch and pulled her back against him. They talked and exchanging funny incidents from their childhood. By mutual unspoken consent, the current situation was off limits tonight.

Gary yawned and eleven and she took the cue and kissed him goodnight and went out the door. "I love you," he said.

Harold was where she expected to find him, passed out in the recliner. But she noticed he looked better and smelled a heck of a lot better.

***

As usual, he called at her break. "Hi beautiful lady, have I ever mentioned I love you?"

"Not since I left you last night. Hello handsome and I love you. Have you heard from Harold today?"

"No, I left him on the floor as usual when I came to work."

"Are you going to his house as we discussed?" she asked.

"Not now. I have a board meeting in an hour. After that, I'll go check on him and call you at the apartment."

"I'll be there, waiting."

A few seconds later her phone rang again. "Where are the keys to my car?" Harold demanded loudly.

"I hid them so you'll sober up. You must be sober tomorrow and go to the bank."

"Who were you taking with, it was busy? You know I call at this time when I need something."

The bank again, they were concerned about you. They said you were told to go to work tomorrow for a meeting."

"What did you tell them?" he demanded.

"The truth, you've been on a binge since the picnic, but they knew that already."

"Where are the car keys," he yelled. "I need them."

"You don't need to drive in your condition. You might kill somebody."

"I'm sober now."

"Then listen to me. A lot of people say you have to hit bottom before you'll admit being an alcoholic. Being fired and broke and me gone appears to be what it'll take for you to realize you have a problem."

She took a deep breath and with sincere meaning, she said, with firmness in her tone that she didn't really feel. She was experiencing fear at what his reaction will be.

"Harold, it's over between us. It ended the day of the picnic. I'm filing for divorce. Forget about me, go on with your life, get professional help."

"You are not going to leave me, ever," he screamed. "That's a promise, I'll kill you first."

Her blood turned to ice at his threatening words. She knew him well enough to know he could be serious. In his mental state, he could kill her. She dropped it, afraid to say more. "I'll bring something nourishing home. You have to eat, but nothing to drink. Do you hear me?"

He hung up.

She called Gary. He answered on the first ring and when he heard her voice he knew something was wrong. "What happened?" he asked.

"Harold called, mad, very mad. He threatened me for the first time. I mean a serious threat. He scared me. I'm afraid he means it."

"Tell me what he said, exactly."

"I'll go back to how it came up so you'll know. I told him a lot of people say you have to hit bottom before admitting to being an alcoholic. I told him that being fired

62

and broke and me gone appeared to be what it would take for him to realize he has a problem. I said I was filing for a divorce. That was when he threatened me. He said I wasn't going to leave him, ever, that's a promise. He said he would kill me first."

"He was sober enough to mean it. Like you said, he's fallen deeper. I don't know him anymore. He sounded like an animal, a mad dog. He has weapons, at one time he was an avid hunter."

"I'm going there now," Gary said. But I'll take somebody with me. As his employer, we're going to check on him, concerned for his safety, since he hasn't reported for work."

"What about your board meeting?" she asked.

"If I'm not back, I'll cancel it, this is more important."

"What do I do?" she asked.

"Can you stay there until I call? I don't want you out on the street. Not after that threat."

"Of course, that's not a problem. I can stay for a while; they won't lock the doors until after the maintenance people finish. That'll be about five. I can use the time to pack my personal things for the end of school."

"Can you lock your door?" he asked.

"I can do that and there are locks on the outside doors. As soon as everybody is gone, I can ask one of the maintenance men to lock the door to the hallway my room is located on."

"Do it. Maybe, just a precaution, but if Harold comes there, he couldn't corner you in your room. I'll call or be there before five. If you see him, call 911, and then call me."

"Yes sir," she said with a groan.

Gary and Marvin drove to Harold's home. Gary brought Marvin up to speed on the situation, that is, about Harold's abuse problem and not reporting for work. Marvin already knew. The whole bank knew. Harold had been the major topic at breaks and lunch since the picnic.

Gary parked in front of the house and sat looking for a minute. "It looks quiet, let's go see."

They went to the front door and he rang the bell, and

Marvin walked to a window. "Nothing," he said. "It looks empty; at least, I don't see Harold.

Gary held the button down for a full minute, hoping if Harold was asleep, this would wake him. When that didn't work, he knocked loudly.

Marvin walked to the garage and peeked in the window. "Empty," he shouted.

Gary swore under his breath, he knew Sarah hid the car keys and Harold's car should be there. "Go around that way and see if you can see anything in a window," he said. "I'll go this way and meet you in back."

He tried to look in windows, but they were covered with curtains or drapes. He met Marvin at the patio door, he was looking inside. His hands were cupped against the glass with his face inside his hands to shield his eyes from the sun's glare.

"Somebody trashed the house," he said. "Come look."

Gary hurried to the glass door. Tables were turned over, dishes were broken as if somebody flung them from the cabinets, food from the refrigerator and freezer was on the floor with their doors standing open.

He tried the door handle and the sliding door opened. "Stay here, I'm going to have a peek inside to make sure he isn't here, passed out, or worse." He knew better, Harold wasn't here, but it offered Marvin a reason for Gary going inside. He really wanted see the condition of the house so he could tell Sarah."

Marvin stepped back and Gary went in and made a quick walk down the hallway. He found the master bedroom a disaster; it was in worse shape than the other part of the house. Every drawer was open and the contents dumped on the floor. The clothing in the closet was scattered.

He reached for his cell and called Sarah. "Harold's not here, his car's gone," he said. "The patio door was open and I'm inside and the house is trashed, your bedroom is awful, everything from the drawers and closet is on the floor. Where did you hide the car keys?"

"I put them in a red purse on the shelf in the closet. They were inside a compartment inside it."

"I see a small red purse, black scroll work on the side, leather."

"That's it," she groaned.

He picked it up and looked inside; the zippered compartment was ripped out.

"Harold found the keys," he said.

"What do I do now?" she asked, concern etched in her voice. "Do you want me to stay here or leave?"

"Come here immediately, but make doubly sure Harold isn't waiting at your car. I recommend you call the police and tell them what happened. Maybe they can find him before he does something stupid and hurts somebody or himself."

"Should I call the police now?" she asked.

"Yes, immediately. Marvin is with me, we'll be parked in front."

"I'm ready to leave. I'll be there as soon as I can."

"Call the police, and then call me back and stay on the phone and check the parking lot before you show yourself. Make sure he's not waiting for you. I expect he went for booze, but we can't take a chance. Keep talking to me as you go to your car."

The maintenance man opened the door and she peeked outside. Her car was the only one in the lot. "All clear," she said.

"Good, but make sure he's not parked nearby waiting or hidden on the other side of your car where you can't see him until he jumps out. Don't speed. It's not going to change anything if you are five minutes longer getting here."

Gary went back to the patio door and closed it. "We'll wait in the car. Sarah called the police."

"I'm in my car," she said, "and on the way. There is no sign of Harold. You were right, he went to a liquor store."

She arrived first and stopped in the driveway. "Stay here," Gary said as he opened his car door. Marvin was about to get out.

Gary hurried to meet Sarah and saw fear on her face. He desperately wanted to pull her into his arms and comfort her, but refrained, two of her neighbors were in their yard watching.

65

"I know," she said, seeing his face. "I want your arms around me, but not now, and the police are on the way."

A police car arrived a few seconds later and stopped behind her car. Two men in uniform stepped out and the driver hurried to them. "Are you Sarah Nance?" he asked.

"Yes, I called you."

The officer looked at Gary. "And you?"

"Gary Justice, I'm Harold's employer."

"I thought you looked familiar. You own the bank."

Gary nodded. "We had a founder's day picnic. Harold drank too much and we had to carry him home. When he didn't report for work, I called Sarah at work. She said he's been hitting the bottle since the picnic. I came here and he was gone, but the house has been trashed."

"I was afraid he would go for more alcohol," Sarah put in. "I hid his car keys. He found them, his car's not here."

"I see," the policeman said. "Can we go inside?"

"Of course." She opened the front door.

"Do you want me to come with you or wait in the car?" Gary asked.

"Wait in your car," the policeman replied quickly. His partner was standing beside their car talking on the radio.

"I ran the information," he said. "I have the license number and description of Mr. Nance's car."

"Come with me," his partner said. "We'll check the house first."

They walked in with Sarah behind them, even though Sarah knew what to expect, she gasped at the destruction. The two policemen took the lead down the hallway. Their hand on their weapon.

"I hid his keys in a red purse in the closet in the bedroom." They found the purse on the bed where Gary put it. "That's it," she said, pointing with her index finger.

"When did you last talk or see your husband?"

"Mr. Justice called me at school about an hour ago, I teach. He said Harold didn't report to work again. Harold called me not more than a minute after I finished talking with Mr. Justice. "He demanded to know where I hid his keys. He threatened me. From his tone of voice, I'm afraid of him.

He threatened to kill me."

"What did he say," the policeman asked. "Tell us about the threat?"

"I made a comment that he might have to hit bottom before he admitted he has an abuse problem. I said something like him being fired, broke and me gone. I told him I was filing for a divorce. Harold said he would kill me first."

"Then what happened?"

"I called Mr. Justice at the bank and told him that Harold was at home and about the threat. He said he would come here. A few minutes later, he called and told me about the house and that Harold wasn't here. He advised me to call you. I'm afraid Harold will do something stupid. He can't be reasoned with when he's drinking. He could hurt somebody or himself. I'm not sure he had enough money to buy liquor," she paused. "He may try to, well, get it anyway he can. When he's out of alcohol, he becomes irrational, he panics, he goes out of control."

The two policemen led the way outside and hurried to their car. Gary saw her standing on the porch, her face white and drawn. He jumped from his car and raced to her and put his arm around her shoulder. The policemen were standing outside their car, talking, and then the man in charge grabbed the radio.

Suddenly, the other policeman hurried to them. "Somebody just robbed a liquor store near here. We have to go. Mrs. Nance, do you have any place you can go? It wouldn't be wise to stay here until this is resolved."

Gary replied quickly. "I'll take care of her. There's no telling what Harold will do." He reached for a card and wrote his cell number on it. Call me when you know something. He handed the officer his card. He didn't want them to know he was taking her to his apartment.

The policeman hurried back to their car and sped away, lights flashing and sirens blaring.

He went to his car where Marvin waited, standing outside watching the activity. "Take my car back to the bank and park it in my space. Leave the keys on my desk. Tell them what happened, and I won't be back today. Advise Tom Boyd I said for him to chair the board meeting."

He led Sarah to her car and opened the passenger side door and helped her sit. He went to the other side and sat behind the wheel and backed out on the street. "Where are you taking me?" she asked.

He met her face with a big smile. "Home."

She glanced back at the house. "That's never going to be my home, again."

Her emotions overflowed for the first time and the tears flowed. Her crying became more intense.

He stopped in front of a store and took her into his arms. This brought on more crying. He stroked her hair and held her close, realizing she needed to unleash her pent-up emotions. He held her, offering soothing comments until her crying finally slowed and turned to sobs. "Unbuckle and sit beside me," he said.

She slid close and his arm circled her shoulder as he drove.

He parked in front of his apartment and hurried to her side and opened the door. They walked to the apartment together, he was holding her arm. She went in first and waited for him to close the door behind her.

"What will I do," she asked, her breath was ragged.

With gentle fingers, he touched her chin and lifted so he could see her face and eyes. "First, we sit at the bar, have a drink, talk and wait for the phone."

He led her to a chair and she dutifully sat and watched him mix a stout drink. She took it from his hand with an appreciative smile.

"Sip it. It's strong," he said.

Gary mixed his and came around and sat beside her and reached for her hand. "This was going to happen. We both knew it. It was only a matter of time and you know this better than me. You saw his condition more than me. He was in a headfirst dive, almost in a free fall. I hope he doesn't hurt anybody before they take him into custody. If he was the one that robbed the liquor store, well, that'll get him off the street for a time. We can only play it as it happens."

"Do I sleep here tonight?" she asked. "The police and all the neighbors, and the condition of my bedroom."

"Yes, you can have the guest bedroom if you want. Sarah, I want you to move here. You can't go back as long as Harold is loose. You'll be safe here."

He met her eyes, for the first time he saw something besides remorse and fear. "Yes sir. You still want me, in spite of what happened?"

"More than ever, if that's possible. We belong together. We need each other. I damn sure know I need you."

She recognized the sincerity in his voice and knew in her heart he loves her. She already knew she was his woman, and eventually will be his wife, and mother of their children. She knew she will be a good wife, caring, loving, and a splendid mother for their children. But several blue thoughts hovered in the background, their relationship is still young and Harold lurking in the darkness. The stress of their meeting and the pressure of her situation. Will Gary feel the same in the days and years to come? Did she bring danger to Gary when he finds out about Gary?

He saw her in deep, serious thought. "Care to share those thoughts with me? I saw something wonderful flash across your face and your eyes sparkled. Then a dark cloud."

Lowering her head she fixed her eyes on her hands on the bar, she spoke, softly and slowly. "I was thinking how lucky I am, a man like you caring and wanting me. I'll be the best I can be, at whatever you want from me." She raised her eyes to meet his. "Your woman, your lover, and should it evolve, someday, your wife and mother of our children. But, are you sure you want me, I mean forever? I may have put you in danger from Harold. When he learns I am with you, he may resort to violence against you."

His eyes glazed over with moisture as he sat, studying her face. His gentle hand pulled her up with him. "Bring your drink."

They walked to the couch, and as before, he sat and she lay back in his arms, comfortable, happy, in spite of the situation. One arm circled under her breast and the other stroked her hair and face, touching her ears and cheek.

69

"Now the dark thought," he said. "Why did you ask the question about me wanting you forever?"

She was honest. "We met in a stressful time in my live. Our romance has been torrid. My thought was, how will you feel in the future, a few years from now, when the passion and newness of our relationship has passed?"

"An easy question to answer, the same as now, looking forward to each day with you, I truly want you as my wife the rest of my life. I searched until I found the woman of my dreams. I expect and want you as my soul mate as long as we live. I know you will make me happy each day of our lives. Seeing you beautiful face at the breakfast table every morning and feeling you snuggled against me at night is what we can expect. I need you to stand at my side as we go through life."

His caresses weren't intended to excite her or arouse passion, they were gentle touches of affectionate and endearment. She knew without a doubt, he wanted her as his partner, companion, but more important, his friend, and someday wife. The sexual relationship would be a bonus, the desert.

She knew she was in love with him since the beginning, but now, he had evolved into being the other half of her life, without him, mere existence would be meaningless.

They sipped their drinks and enjoyed the quiet moments together, away from the world. Away from her situation and Harold.

She felt the effects of the drink, but she was not even close to being drunk, but it helped her relax and come down from her tense emotional state. "I feel a little giddy," she said. "I skipped lunch, worried, I don't eat under stress. The last thing I ate was toast for breakfast."

He helped her stand and led her back to the bar, and then he went into the kitchen, and made a pot of coffee. She sat and watched him make a ham and cheese sandwich. He cut it into four parts and put a double helping of potato chips on the plate. He placed it in front of her. "Every bite young lady. You need food and the grease in the chips will coat your stomach."

She took a bite, suddenly realizing she was hungry. He

70

made another sandwich for himself and put it on the bar and filled two large cups with coffee.

As she ate, she watched his face. Not one hint of negative thoughts crossed his mind. He read her mind. "As soon as this is resolved, will you file for divorce? I want the past left behind and you and I can start our lives. Will you marry me as soon as you can legally do so?"

She wanted to say yes, but held it in check. Instead of replying, as she wanted, she hedged. "Please understand, we've known each other such a short time. I'll marry you when the time's right, but not now. I made one horrible mistake in my life. I admit, I'm a little gun-shy. I'll live with you, we'll be together, as a couple, after a time, then if there's any reservation or concern, either can walk away, no ties, no legal ramifications. We give our relationship a fair chance to bloom or die."

"Then," she said as her eyes began to mist, "if we both know it's right, ask and I'll be your wife. "I'll happily walk beside you."

He sat looking into her very being through her eyes and touched a tiny tear on her cheek with his index finger. "I made a horrible mistake Connie and can relate to your fear. I had fear of another marriage, well, that is, until I met you. That fear faded before that first night ended. I understand the stress you are under now, and I agree with your request. I'll wait for you to tell me when the time is right. Until then, we manage as best as we can with Harold."

She shivered at that negative though, knowing it's probable the worst is yet to come.

"Please do exactly what I ask you to do and we'll see it through," he said. "I'll make sure you're safe. I love you. I love you with all my heart. And I'm going to protect you."

She clutched his hand. "This is the way it should be between a woman and her man. If Harold ever said he loved me, I didn't remember it. Maybe he said it, like people say good morning, but he never said it, meaning it, like you say, I love you. I know it comes from your heart and not from your loins or greed for something, like money."

The ringing of his cell phone caused both to jump. He

71

pulled his phone with his eyes on her. "Gary Justice speaking," he said.

"This is patrolman Lewis. It wasn't Harold that robbed the liquor store. We caught the perp and have a positive ID from three eye witnesses, as well as the security camera. He was a young punk and a known addict. There's no word on Harold's whereabouts."

"Thank you," Gary said. "Keep me posted, I'll protect Sarah."

She heard the policeman and felt relief. "I heard. It wasn't Harold. I don't know whether to be happy or sad. For his sake, he needs help and he isn't going to get it until he's forced. But at least, he didn't rob the store and nobody was hurt."

"I agree with you," he said.

"What's a perp, the policeman used that word?"

"A perp in their lingo is perpetrator."

"Of course, I should have known that."

"Harold is a perp in our lives," he said.

"I'm sorry," she whispered.

"I didn't mean it the way it came out. Think about this. If it hadn't been for Harold, I wouldn't have met you."

"How do you know that?" she asked. "What if Harold had been sober and we were at the picnic and we were introduced. Would the giant magnets inside us have pulled us together?"

"God woman, that magnet inside you attracted me to you from a long distance. I saw you and couldn't, or didn't want to take my eyes off of you."

"I'm glad. The same goes for you. When our eyes met, I felt you pulling me to you."

"I have only one conclusion," he said. "We were meant for each other." His arms tightened around her.

"Yes," she whispered.

"Yes," he repeated, "why did you say that?"

"Because you asked me if I wanted to go to bed and make love?"

"I was thinking that, but I didn't say it, did I?"

"I don't know if it was said aloud or not, but I heard it

72

as clear as everything."

"I hope by the time your divorce is final you know the time is right and we can set the date and you can start selecting your wedding dress."

"That's possible," she said. "When will we start on our family?"

"About thirty minutes after the reception," he teased.

Her cell phone rang. Her happy mood suddenly went south. She pushed the button and waited as she took a deep breath. "Hello," she said.

"As before, she was greeted with a string of cuss words. "Where in the hell are you?" he shouted.

"Not at home, that's for damn sure after what you did to the house."

"It's your fault," he yelled. "For hiding the keys. My credit cards wouldn't work and they wouldn't take a check. What did you do?"

"I cancelled the cards and moved the money out of the account. Otherwise you would spend it all on booze."

Another string of cuss words stung the air. "I only had enough money to buy a pint of the cheapest gin they had. You'll pay for this."

"Where are you?" she demanded.

"At home."

"Then clean up the mess you made or live in the squalor. I don't care. You can drink the pint and pass out again, but when you wake up, I won't be there and you'll be broke."

Gary was holding her hand; his strength was keeping her strong. She took a deep breath. "I'm filing for divorce and I won't be back, except for my clothing and what's mine."

Silence hung heavy for a long moment. "That'll be a cold day in hell. I'll kill you before I grant you a divorce. You're a dead woman walking."

The phone went dead.

Gary put his gentle hand on her cheek and turned her so he could see her face. "Tomorrow, I'm getting you away from here. I don't think he's making idle threats and I'm not taking any chances with him hurting you. He sounded sober."

Her phone rang again. "You're with another man," he said.

"I won't lie. I'm in his arms and he loves me and I love him. I'm going to marry him after the divorce is final."

"Who is he?" Harold demanded.

She ignored the question. "I'll be with him where you'll never find me. Sober up and get help and go on with your life. It's over between us. I don't love you and I'm getting out while I can, before you have the opportunity to do something stupid. You have threatening to kill me, twice."

"Are you sleeping with him?" he demanded.

"Not yet, but I will."

"I'll find out who he is and you just signed a death warrant for both of you. You'll be together, but in a grave. You on the bottom, face down and he'll be lying on his back, on top of you."

Fear surged through her, but she maintained strength in her voice, mostly because of Gary's steel embrace. "Harold, leave me alone. Go find another life. Ours is finished. You know this as well as I do. It's been over between us for several years. You don't love me and I don't love you. We have been strangers sharing the same house, but no more. It ended the day of the picnic."

She touched the end button with her finger, and then the off button.

Gary turned her in his arms and held her and she clung to him, unafraid.

"He knows where you teach," Gary said. "You can't go there tomorrow, he might be waiting. You'll have to report in sick. Besides, tomorrow is the last day of school."

"I can't do that to my students, or the school."

"What if he comes to the school with a gun? What if he starts shooting at you, think about your students in that case."

She began to cry. He held her and stroked her shoulders and back. "If it's that important to you, I'll go with you."

Sarah looked at him, her crying stopped at his statement

and fear took its place. "I'm not going to put you in danger because of me. Harold has slipped over the edge. You heard him and he will kill you if given the chance. This is my problem. I appreciate your offer, but please understand. I couldn't stand it if he hurt you because of me."

"You're the one that doesn't understand. It's our problem now. I love you too much to let that stupid drunk ruin our lives. I was in the service, special forces. Should he come to the school, I'll handle him. He won't hurt you, your students, or me. I promise."

She gasped at his words. "Gary, oh lord. I've never known a man like you."

His strong secure arms clutched the most precious woman in the world. His love for her radiated and warmed her.

He stood and lifted her into his arms and took her to the bedroom. She kissed him with all the love a woman can have for her man. They clung together during the night, they didn't make love, passion wasn't the need they shared. He held her in his arms where she belongs, safe and secure from Harold and the unpleasant things of life.

***

He woke her early with a kiss. She opened her eyes and returned the kiss.

His gentle fingers caressed her cheek. "A big day for us. We need to dress and eat a hardy breakfast."

She rolled from the bed and reached for his hand.

He finished dressing and went to the closet and come back with a .38 pistol in a leather holster. He shoved it in the small of his back and covered it with his shirt.

Worry and fear was fixed on her face. She cringed. "Please be careful. If you hurt or kill Harold, you'll be arrested."

"I'll think with my brain, not my emotions. If I did something stupid, he would win. I fully intend for our life together began last night when you came to my bed. I'm not taking any chances on losing you. I have license to carry a concealed weapon, if that's one of your concerns?"

"It was, thank you. But even so, that doesn't give you

license to use it. I'm scared, Harold could come at you or us and you would be forced to kill him. The police could arrest you. The grand jury may call it self-defense, but the publicity, and it would come out about us. I could see the headlines in the paper, Gary Justice, Sarah Nance's lover, kills her husband."

He welcomed her trembling body into his arms and held her close. She shivered even more. "Darling, relax and trust me," he said. "I'll be careful and only use my weapon as a last resort. But I'll be there in case he twists off and comes to the school after you. In fact, I'm going to report Harold's threat to the police. They know about him after the incident. I expect I can talk them into sending a car to the school."

That helped her emotions. "Thank you, let them handle it. Even in self-defense, would it put something between us? I mean you shooting, or killing Harold. You know what I mean."

"I do and I won't, except to protect you and the children."

Gary called the police station and asked to speak with the sergeant in charge. "This is Gary Justice. Do you know about the incident involving an employee of my bank, Harold Nance, he trashed his house looking for the car keys his wife hid to keep him from driving to buy more booze?"

"I recall that incident," the sergeant said.

"Harold threatened his wife when she told him she was filing for divorce. He said he would kill her first. This is the last day of school and we are concerned he'll go there with a weapon. Sarah said he was an avid hunter and owns guns. I called hoping you could have a car there just in case."

"Was he drunk when he made the threat?"

"I'm sure he was drinking. Drunk, I don't know. He hasn't been sober since the bank picnic. He hasn't reported to work and he's been on a continuing binge."

"Mr. Justice, if I sent a car to every threat, I wouldn't have near enough men."

"I can appreciate that," Gary agreed with honesty. "But think about this. I've warned you of possible violence, involving a man under the influence and threading to kill his wife and has weapons. He knows she'll be at the school today, at a public school where there'll be a lot of small children. He's out of control and should he barge into the school grounds or classroom shooting, it could evolve into total carnage."

He stopped speaking and let that thought soak in before adding more arguments.

"I understand. Does she have to report today?"

"I asked her the same thing. She said it's the last day of school and she owes it to her students and the administration. I can appreciate that, but even if she didn't go, Harold wouldn't know, and he could still barge into the school with a pistol in his hand. Besides, even if he didn't, if he's hell bent on violence, he would find her somewhere else and kill her. Wouldn't it be better to end it now, take him into custody, and seek professional help for him?"

"You make your point Mr. Justice. I'll have a car with two of my best detectives at the school and escort her into the school building and have a patrol car posted in the parking lot in case Harold comes later."

"Thank you," Gary said. "I'm going to drive her and I'm going to be armed, just in case."

"Mr. Justice, that isn't necessary."

"I hope not, but I have a license to carry, and I have training. I won't draw my weapon unless it's absolutely necessary to protect Sarah and the children. That nut may have a rifle and attack from a distance, or come in shooting wildly. He's out of control and isn't thinking coherently due to alcohol abuse."

"If he does," the sergeant said, "my men can handle it."

"I hope so, but I'm going to be armed, and I'll meet your men at the entrance to the school." He looked at the clock. "At eight o'clock."

"I'll have them there, but you stay out of it."

"I will if your men handle the problem, but if not, as I said, I'm going to protect Sarah and the children."

He ended the call.

"Thank you," she whispered and smiled at him. "I'm sorry I'm causing you trouble," she said.

"For your and our sake I want this to end," he said. "I want to end it today and get on with our lives. We're going to the ranch and I want to be able to relax and hold my beautiful Sarah in my arms without fear."

She lifted her face and buried it against his neck.

Chapter 7

Harold held the pint of gin in his hands, and then turned it up and drained it. With a shudder, he tossed the empty bottle toward the trash. For the first time in days he felt hungry. He went to the kitchen and saw all the food he had thrown on the floor was spoiled. He found a can of chili and an unbroken bowel and heated it in the microwave. While it warmed, he went through the pantry and located a box of crackers on the floor. He sat at the bar and ate every bite. He cursed as he ate, Sarah should be here cooking for him. Secretly, he couldn't blame her for wanting to divorce him. But, he couldn't stand the humiliation of her divorcing him to marry another man. His ego was too large to accept her finding somebody better.

He stood and went to his bedroom knowing the binge was over for him. He walked to the bathroom and looked at himself in the mirror and frowned at his appearance. With a scowl, he headed for the shower and soaped his body, and then stood with hot water cascading over his head and shoulders. The water finally turned cool and he stepped out and reached for a towel.

He dressed in shorts and a knit shirt and went to the bar and sat down. He wanted a drink, but shrugged his shoulders, and picked up a pen and scratch pad.

Who could Sarah's lover be? he thought. His first thought, the pastor of the church, or the music director. She attended regularly offering her the opportunity. It was always mid afternoon when she got home from church. What did she do during that time?

He wrote preacher and music, and then considered the preacher first. Happily married from what he recalled her saying, besides, he remembered her saying he was only about five foot seven, she would never consider a man shorter than her. A phobia of long standing for her. The music director, after thinking about him for a minute, he rejected that choice. He was over sixty.

He scratched both and turned his attention to her school. The principal jumped into his mind. She had stated several times she liked him much more than the principal that retired at the end of last year. Since he couldn't remember his name, he went to a pile of papers from her desk that he dumped on the floor. He spotted a letter from the school. Billy Swan, and put that name on his list.

Next, the physical education teacher. Harold had met him a few times, tall, well over six foot and with an athlete's body. He remembered his name, Norman Wagner. One more name on the list. A fellow teacher she had attended several meeting with, in fact, he recalled they spent a couple of days at a workshop at the service center. Benton, but his first name eluded him. Then he recalled, Carl, called, Bud. Bud Benton's name was entered on the list.

Harold couldn't think of anybody else at the school she had mentioned since most of the teachers in the elementary school were female. His mind explored other possible men she knew.

His best friend, Tommy Hall, now divorced. Tommy had been to their home several times and Sarah enjoyed dancing with him. He remembered seeing them dance for hours, but that had been years ago. He and Tommy had a major disagreement over something and he hadn't seen Tommy in a couple of years. But that didn't mean Sarah had also broken off the friendship. He added Tommy to his list.

After exploring all the possibilities, he had a dozen names on his list. The bank came to mind, he couldn't think of anybody. Sarah didn't know the employees. He never took her to a function, except the annual founder's day picnic and Christmas party.

Only one name came to mind, Gary Justice, but then she didn't know him, except she had mentioned he and Marvin helped load him in the car after the picnic. She mentioned he called, asking about him, but if he was her lover, she wouldn't dare mention his name. He didn't add

Gary to his list.

He went back over the twelve names and ranked them. Billy Swan, the principal, Norm Wagner, the P E teacher, Tommy Hall, his ex-friend. If the first three names proved to be wrong, he could pick three more to investigate.

After the chore of selecting possible names as Sarah's lover, he sat, wishing for a drink, but again put that thought aside, and went to the closet and dug into his hunting gear. With care, he unwrapped his pistol. A .45 and a box of ammunition and took them to the bar and began cleaning the weapon. He loaded the clip and put it in a holster and filled the empty spaces on the belt with bullets.

Next, he went to the closet for his deer rifle. A Winchester .306 with a scope. He cleaned and loaded it with care.

He left the weapons on the bar and went to the bedroom and lay down, his mind exploring the best way to catch her with her lover. The school came to mind first, but he waved that off. He wanted them both, preferably, at the same time, he would kill the man first, with her watching, knowing she was next. That thought gave him a thrill, more so than having sex with her. She never excited him. Sex with her was more for a tension release for him, and a wifely obligation to her. She was never passionate, even when they first met and married. He wondered about her and her lover. What did he see in her? It couldn't be sex, since she always lay on her back and endured. A frown on her mouth, she always asked him to hurry. He recalled the last time he tried to have sex with her. It was her fault he couldn't perform.

Harold went to the recliner in the den and pushed back, considering his options. He decided to report for work tomorrow morning and get it over with. He wanted to see if the new owner, Justice was lying about firing him. He began thinking of excuses he hadn't used to tell his co-workers. Justice knew why, but maybe the employees didn't. He fell asleep.

Harold woke early and missed the smell of coffee brewing and bacon frying. Sarah always had breakfast ready for him. She kept a spotless house, made a good salary, and he would miss her, but he couldn't let her get away with leaving him for another man. That thought infuriated him.

He put on his best suit and an ironed shirt, another thing he would miss, she always kept his clothing ready and neat, but then he could send the laundry out.

Feeling better than he expected, he walked to the kitchen and viewed the mess again and made a mental note to hire somebody to clean the house.

The clock read seven-fifteen. He wanted to arrive early, but needed something in his stomach. He found a loaf of bread under the table where he had tossed it and made two pieces of toast and a cup of instant coffee. At ten minutes to eight, he walked into the bank. Everybody turned and stopped what they were doing when he walked through the door.

Marvin saw him and quickly dialed Gary's cell phone. He caught his boss before he reached the school. "Harold Nance just walked into the bank. He's dressed in a nice suit and looking like nothing ever happened."

Gary was stunned.

"What?" Sarah asked, in a whisper.

"Thanks Marvin. I'll be there shortly."

He touched the end button and turned to Sarah. "Harold walked into the bank, dressed in a suit. Marvin said he looked like nothing ever happened."

She gasped in disbelief.

Gary immediately dialed the police station and was put through to the sergeant he talked with about Harold. "I was just advised that Harold Nance reported to work at the bank. A complete surprise to me. I fully expected him to be waiting for his wife at the school."

"As I said," the policeman jabbed, using a, I told you so tone of voice. "Most threats made by men under the influence rarely follow through. In this case, I'm glad, since it could have gotten serious in a hurry if he showed up at the school with a weapon." He wasn't about to cross Mr. Justice. He was an important man, and he had a note at Justice's bank.

"My apologies," Gary said. "I was wrong."

"I can't blame you for being concerned and cautious, your apology isn't needed." Gary hit the end button, looking at her. "When will you finish for the day?"

"I expect about one, we'll dismiss after lunch. What should I do?"

"I'll have Marvin pick you up and take you home. You can change and he'll go with you to your old house. He'll be in his pickup and you take your car. As quickly as possible, move everything you'll need. Using both vehicles, and with his help, you should have most of your things moved quickly. Put them in the apartment, we can go through them and put them away later. I'll keep Harold in sight and should he leave, I'll call you. I don't want him catching you at his house."

She nodded; he was thinking it was Harold's house now, not hers.

"Call me when you're finished moving and I'll meet you at home. I want to put your car in a safe place where Harold can't find it. Pack your bags and I'll pick you up and we'll leave for the ranch."

A worried frown appeared on her face. "I'm still concerned. Are we doing the right thing?"

"We are if you love me?"

"Yes, yes, I love you. More than I can tell you."

"I love you and this is right, we belong together. A few days at the ranch, just us, we can relax, enjoy being together. I have so much to show you. We can lounge and talk a lot. I want to hear about your life and learn every detail about your likes and dislikes."

She reached for his offered hand, a soft smile on her face.

"I can't wait to show you the ranch and your new home," he said with a smile. "It will be where we'll live and raise our children. From here on, the ranch is going to be our home where only love will reside."

A genuine smile spread over her face. Her heart pounded, her spine tingled, her eyes misted and she gave herself to him again without reservations. For the first time in her life, she felt consumed by her love for a man. Her body responded to him and heat radiated, her breast needed his attention.

Panic hit her. Would Abby see her state? Would she know? She felt her love for Gary was as transparent as the expression on her face.

Gary stopped the car at the school and shifted in his seat. She wanted to reach for him, but refrained, children were walking by, and she saw Abby watching. "Your kiss is on hold until it's more private," she said.

"I know, but tonight will be our time. I want your body in our bed where I can touch you."

She wanted to blush, but instead, she beamed. "Stop that. Abby just parked and is coming toward us. She'll see right into me and know."

"Know what?"

"You know damn well what, you enjoy turning me on. Can you see it on my face and in my eyes?"

He made a show of studying her face. "All I can see is the neon sign flashing on your forehead. It says, I love Gary Justice."

She giggled and jumped from the car and rushed toward the building, not wanting to talk with Abby.

Gary waved and drove away.

Abby ran to catch up with Sarah. "That was Gary Justice, why did he bringing you to work?" She was tittering under her breath, and was putting it together. "Oh my god, Sarah. Gary Justice, congratulations. No wonder you're glowing like the star on top of a Christmas tree."

Sarah wanted to shout her happiness. "Harold threatened to kill me. He could have been waiting. Mr. Justice brought me to work, as a precaution."

Abby raised one eyebrow and demanded, "Where did you meet him this morning, or did you sleep with him last night?"

"Abby, you're my friend, right?"

"Of course I am, why?"

"Then keep your mouth shut. I mean it." She didn't bother to deny anything, knowing it would only give more credence to Abby's thoughts.

Abby's face flushed. "It's true, you're sleeping with him." She looked around to see if anybody was close enough to hear. "We have to talk. I want details. Is he good? Is it serious? What did Harold say? Did you tell him about Gary?"

Sarah stomped her foot. "Stop it Abby. No more questions." She hurried away and went toward her classroom. Abby followed at a trot demanding Sarah talk.

Thankfully, students gathered around them and stopped any farther questions. "We'll talk later," Abby said as she turned to go to her room.

"That'll be a cold day in hell," Sarah said under her breath. As soon as school finished, she intended to be out of the building and gone. Marvin would be waiting and she could rush out and jump into his truck before Abby could corner her.

The morning was hectic, the kids were rowdy, excited and anxious for the summer vacation. Her nerves were already frayed with the threat of Harold. Gary's love for her and her feelings for him played around in her mind. Her life was in turmoil.

Lunch time finally arrived. She went with the students to the cafeteria where mothers were waiting and stayed until she saw Marvin arrive. Sarah said her farewell to the kids and hurried to her room for her things.

Marvin saw her at the door and hurried to help her put the boxes in his pickup. Together, they loaded them and she jumped in. "Hurry, before I'm caught by a friend."

Marvin put the pickup in gear and they drove from the parking lot. She looked back and saw Abby standing outside, her hands on her hips, watching Sarah leave.

She turned back to Marvin. "What did Gary tell you?"

"I'm at your disposal. Mr. Justice said you needed to move your things to his apartment."

"Take me to the apartment first. I need to change and unload the school boxes, then we can go to my house for my things. Was Harold still at the bank?"

"Yes, Mr. Justice said he would call if he left. He said he would keep him there as long as he could. He delayed his meeting with Harold on purpose."

"Tell me," she asked, "what do you think of what I'm doing. You have to know. Does everybody at the bank know?"

"Of course I know. Everybody at the bank knows now, but we have vowed to keep it between us. We all know Harold and his temper. The word has spread that he threatened to kill you. Janice's husband is a policeman. He told her about the death threat."

"I think it's wonderful," Marvin added. "I liked you that night at the picnic. I told Mr. Justice you're special. He's an honorable man, a great boss, and he needs a good woman. I hope you two continue. Since he met you his personality has improved and he's happy. When he first came to the bank, he seemed so, well, depressed, despondent and wore a false smile. That has all changed now. We know it's because of you. When he comes in every morning, he whistling a tune and has a genuine smile on his face. Talk about a night and day change in his attitude."

"I feel the same. He has certainly changed my life, for the better. Now let's get busy. He wants me moved into his apartment, or as he says, he wants me to move home. We need to do that before Harold leaves the bank."

Chapter 8

Gary went to Harold's office as soon as he arrived and shook Harold's hand. "I'm happy to see you came to work. I see a stack of mail on your desk. Work through it and see what has come in while you were on leave."

"When are we having the talk you mentioned when you came to my home?" Harold asked.

"I have several things lined up and a meeting. It will be sometime after lunch. You have plenty to keep you busy until I send for you."

"You said I wasn't going to be fired. Is that right?" If you are, why spend the day working when I could leave now?"

"You're not going to be fired, but there are several stipulations and requirements you must agree to do, and you'll be on probation until you carry them out. But not terminated if you comply and meet the requirements."

With that, Gary turned and walked out of Harold's office. He didn't want to get into the details of the stipulations now.

He called Marvin to his office. "Keep an eye on Harold. Make sure he doesn't leave the building. If he does, come get me immediately."

At lunch, Harold asked one of the employees leaving to bring him a burger. He ate in the break room with several employees. The conversation was light and cheery. Nobody wanted to bring up Harold's problem. Nobody was about to mention Gary and Sarah.

He quickly ate his lunch and went to the vault and requested the key to his security box. He opened the door with the two keys, carried the metal box to a table, and stood where nobody could see what he was doing. He opened an envelope to make sure it was the right one, and put it in his coat pocket. He replaced the box and handed the woman the bank key, and put his in his side pocket.

He went back to his office and sat back in his chair. This was the first time he had dipped into his stash of funds. Sarah had transferred their account, and it was a week away from payday.

He had a feeling today would end badly and he wanted his money out of the bank.

It had been over five years since a man came to his office and introduced himself as Mark Holt, an attorney, representing a corporation investing in real estate. The corporation was applying for an interim loan of two hundred thousand. The attorney presented the necessary forms. Everything was in order, except a current appraisal on the property.

Nance mentioned the requirement to Mr. Holt. The attorney reached for an envelope inside his briefcase and handed it to Harold. He looked inside and counted the cash. Three thousand dollars in small bills, mostly twenties. Harold glanced up at the attorney with a passive face.

"Since I'm from out of town," Holt said. "Would you be kind enough to contact an appraiser of your choice? Pay his fee out of that." He pointed toward the envelope. "Keep the remainder for your trouble." Holt stood and turned toward the door. "You have my number if you need additional information, and when you need signatures on the loan documents."

The loan went through without question and Harold put twenty-five hundred dollars in the security box. Two months later, Mark Holt again came to Harold's office with a cashier's check to pay the loan in full including interest.

He presented another application for the purchase of more real estate. This time the loan was for five-hundred thousand. As before, Harold was given money for the appraisal. However, this time the envelope contained seven-thousand.

Harold suspected the reason for the purchases, drug dealers laundering money through the purchase of property, and then pay it off with drug money. With each purchase, a different corporation was the purchaser. The loans became more frequent and the amounts larger.

Harold knew he should report his suspicions, but he had a gut feeling he would need the funds sometime in the future and he could always play it as he had no idea the purchases were for illegal purposes.

Harold now had over a half million stashed.

***

Gary called Marvin into his office and give him orders on going after Sarah. "I'll keep Harold in sight and when he leaves, I'll call Sarah or you. When that happens, take her to my apartment immediately and stay there until I arrive. Do not let Harold near her. Do whatever it takes to protect her. She's very special to me. Lock the door and don't answer it unless it's me. If Harold comes to the apartment dial 911 immediately. If Harold should attempt to break the door down, take Sarah out the back and run like hell."

Gary kept delaying the meeting with Harold until after the bank closed at three. He called Harold's office and asked him to come to the board room at four. That was as long as he could keep him. Sarah should have had ample time to get her things moved.

Gary called her often and assured her Harold was still at the bank and that gave her and Marvin time to make more trips. She took everything she wanted, including a few small pieces of furniture like her grandmother's hutch. She used old quilts to wrap the furniture, but put her antique bedspread in the back seat of her car for the glass wear. Thankfully, her antique china was undamaged when Harold trashed the house.

Marvin was kept busy carrying things from the house to the pickup and her car.

***

At four, Harold tapped on the board room door and Gary invited him inside. Thomas Boyd, the bank president, and Bill Young, the vice-president were there. Gary wanted witnesses to what transpired.

Gary asked Harold to have a chair, and leaned back against the table to talk. "This meeting is to discuss your

89

situation. Your absence from work was approved for sick leave which exceeded you available days. Those days will be carried as a negative balance until they are restored."

Harold didn't comment, so Gary continued. Your conduct at the Founders Day Picnic was deplorable and certainly not the image we maintain for our employees. Families were there, including children."

"Your job performance has been rated unacceptable, and you haven't attempted to improve. In fact, it has taken a steady decline despite you being furnished notices."

"As I told you, you are not going to be terminated, but we have several requirements and stipulations to discuss."

Harold sat with his hands on his lap, listening to Gary Justice.

"First, you will admit yourself to an alcohol abuse clinic."

Harold spoke for the first time. "I'm not an alcoholic. I can stop anytime I choose. Look at me today."

"I agree you are here today, sober. But for the past several months, you've reported to work in good condition, but then for several days, you came to work either drinking or drunk. You have gone to lunch and consumed alcohol, and have a record of being tardy, both in the morning and reporting back to work after lunch."

"I told you that there were several stipulations for retaining your job. The first one is successfully completing rehabilitation at an approved clinic and maintaining abstinence from alcohol for one year. Your work performance must improve to a satisfactory level. You'll be expected to report to work at the required time and remain in your office until the work day is finished. Tardiness in the morning and following lunch will not be tolerated."

Gary paused. "Do you have any questions or comments?"

Harold sat for a few moments before he exploded. "Sarah, my wife has left me for another man. It's all her fault that I drank. It was her fault I didn't report for work, she didn't wake me. I don't have an alcohol dependency. You'll find that out soon enough."

90

He stood and verbally lashed. "You think you are all so goddamned important. I'll show you Harold Nance can't be pushed around. He picked up the chair and threw it at the three men. The men were able to catch it before it hit them. Harold stormed to the door and kicked it open, shattering it into splinters. The employees still in the bank scrambled for cover. They saw Harold was out of control.

"Do we call the police?" Young asked.

Gary shook his head. "Not now. We could have him detained, but hopefully, he'll get control of his emotions and realize we are trying to help him. If he's arrested and put in jail, it would only be for a short time, and then he would be out, madder than he is now. He could do something stupid and resort to extreme violence."

"I've had experiences with men in his condition," Boyd injected. "I'm afraid he may twist off and do something ugly. He may come to the bank with a gun or catch any of us and start shooting. I recommend we notify the police and have him picked up. When they see his mental state, he may be admitted without his consent. My opinion, this is the course of action we should take."

Billy Young was nodding his agreement. "I agree with Thomas. I vote to notify the police."

Gary felt they were right, but didn't want to be the one to report him. He had done so earlier, but didn't want to tell them. He relented, secretly relieved.

Gary hurried to his office and called Sarah. She and Marvin were at his apartment. He gave her a brief synopsis of what happened. "I'll be home as soon as I can. Did you get everything moved?"

"With Marvin's help, I got everything, but it's in a pile in your, I mean our apartment."

"That's okay. We'll sort it out later. Stay there until I get there. Tell Marvin to stay with you and keep watch. Where is your car?"

"Parked in the drive. Marvin's pickup is parked behind it."

"I doubt Harold will come there, but I don't want to take the chance of him driving by and seeing it. Pack what you want to take to the ranch today. Have Marvin put it in your car. We're taking both. But, you won't be coming back until the situation with Harold is resolved. You'll be much safer there."

He hung up and went back to the boardroom. It was empty. He found Boyd and Young in the president's office. Boyd was on the phone, talking with the police.

"The police will be on the lookout for him," Bill Young said. "They knew his name the minute Thomas told them."

"I know. They went to his house when he trashed it and this morning they were staked out at Harold's wife's school where she teaches. He threatened to kill her."

It may come out now about he and Sarah, it couldn't be helped due to the circumstances. Neither asked any questions. They both knew about Gary and Sarah.

"I'm leaving town for the long weekend," Gary said. "I'll see you Tuesday."

They knew he was going to the ranch, even though he didn't mention it.

Gary hurried out of the bank and jumped in his car. He was cautious and kept glancing back. He spotted a car tailing him and knew it had to be Harold. He slowed and made the light on yellow. The car behind him raced through the red light. A police car parked at the intersection sped after Harold. Harold saw the flashing lights behind him and tried to escape, but the police car was able to cut him off. Harold jumped out and thought about racing toward a store, but another police car was in the way.

Gary parked and watched. He wanted to know if they took Harold into custody.

Harold was escorted to a police car. Gary couldn't keep from smiling. He called the bank and advised Boyd of the incident. "Don't file charges. The publicity could hurt the bank's image more than filing would accomplish. Harold would be out in a matter of hours and as we discussed, he could turn violent."

He hurried home to Sarah.

Marvin came out to meet him and he saw Sarah peeking out the door. "Everything is okay," he said with a reassuring smile. "I'll tell you about it later."

Marvin put a few boxes in Gary's car that wouldn't fit in hers while Gary held Sarah in his arms and kissed her trembling lips.

As soon as Gary had everything he would need at the ranch loaded, he gave Marvin and Sarah a thumbnail sketch of what transpired at the bank. When he relayed the subsequent happening with the police, Sarah listened with her hand over her mouth.

Gary thanked Marvin and shook his hand. "Marvin, I appreciate your help today and at the picnic. I can see a bright future in the bank. Keep up the good work and you will advance. A smiling Marvin wished them the best, then hopped in his pickup and left.

Justice got in his car and drove toward the highway with Sarah following close behind. As soon as he was on the highway, he called her on her cell phone.

He didn't go into any more detail over the phone. "We'll have plenty of time to talk later. Like seventy or more years."

Chapter 9

It was after dark when they arrived at the ranch. She couldn't see anything in the car lights, except a house constructed of large white rock. He stopped and hurried back to her car. She opened the door and stepped out in time for him to lift her in his arms and carry her to the house.

He had to put her down to find the key in his pocket, then reached inside, and flipped a switch. He lifted her again and carried her inside.

"I'm practicing carrying you over the threshold when we marry," he said, almost seriously.

A spacious den greeted them with a huge fireplace along one wall. The floor was made of hardwood, though worn in the heavy traffic areas, but it was varnished and polished to a shine. An area Indian rug covered the space between a brown leather couch and the hearth. A matching recliner and two end tables completed the furniture in front of the massive fireplace.

At the other end of the den, a table-high bar separated the kitchen from the den. Four sturdy leather padded chairs were around the bar. An antique chandelier offered lightning for the den, but hidden recessed lighting supplemented the main fixture. A wet bar was against a wall with a huge window behind it.

Gary let her look before he carried her down the hallway. He entered a bedroom at the end of the hallway. It was huge. It was furnished with polished cedar furniture including an entertainment center of the same wood with a large screen television and the usual electronic devices. The post on the bed were massive, and at least five feet tall. A holster with a pistol hung from one of them.

Sarah saw the letter J burned into the headboard.

He saw her looking at it. He spoke for the first time

94

since entering the house. "That has been the brand since the inception of the ranch. The bed and chest of drawers are the original furniture from when the house was built by my great-grandfather. I know it's overpowering, but it has sentimental affection for me. The weapon belonged to my great-grandfather and I was told he never left the house without it on his hip. It's been there on the bedpost all my life."

Without putting her down, he carried her into the bathroom. The room was spacious, equipped with a sauna, a hot tub, as well as a standard tub and shower. The tub and shower were double the normal size. A vanity extended the length of the bathroom with a mirror to the ceiling behind it. The floor was polished marble.

He let her look, and then turned and pushed a door open. A closet the size of most bed rooms was empty, except for his clothing, which used only a small portion of one side. "Will this be sufficient for your clothing if we decide to use this bedroom?"

She spoke for the first time. "I saw three more doors as we came down the hallway. Are they bedrooms?"

"Yep, I'll show them to you."

They were furnished with conventional furniture. The flooring was thick pile carpet and both had a king size bed. They were both larger than normal bedrooms. "We can convert one or two to nurseries if you want. That is, when the time comes."

Her emotions were in high gear.

"Now the rest of the tour," he said.

He carried her back to the den and opened a door. She saw a playroom equipped with exercise equipment and a pool table. Another wet bar was on one side and an entertainment center on the other. A large picture window was at the end of the room covered by drapes.

"Tomorrow, you can see the spring fed pond from this window. Wildlife come here to drink. There's a covered deck that's a good place to enjoy an evening cocktail and come down from a stressful day. It's also a great place for breakfast as well."

"Behind this house are three homes. Two for the

cowboys, and the other for the maintenance man. He takes care of the grounds and makes necessary repairs to the house, the barn, and corral. His wife is the housekeeper and cooks for me when I'm at home."

She gave him a hug before speaking. "I consider that to be my job now. I feel a woman should cook for her man, but I may call on her for help. Especially after the children are here."

"Of course, anytime you need help."

"Are you hungry?" she asked. "I am and I know you didn't eat lunch."

"I notified Juan that I was coming home and for Maria to cook something for us. She's anxious to meet you. She said she was eager to have another woman here. Neither of the cowboys are married."

He carried her to the kitchen and put her down and opened the refrigerator. There were several covered bowels. Sarah began taking them out and putting them on the counter.

She uncovered the meal and began heating steak and vegetables while he mixed them a cocktail. In addition to the meal, she found a pecan pie on the counter. The meal looked appetizing.

***

Sarah joined him on the couch and sipped her drink and began to relax. Occasionally, she went to the kitchen to check on the food. When it was ready, he set the table. Garry helped her sit and took the chair at the end of the bar. He reached for her hand and offered a prayer.

Even though the food had been warmed, it was delicious. They were both hungry. She found ice cream in the freezer and scooped a generous portion on his pie and a small amount on hers.

They went back to couch and she sat beside him. His cell phone rang. It was Boyd from the bank. "I thought you should know. Harold Nance is out of on his personal recognizance. All they had on him was my report and running a stop light. The other items never came to pass. If he wanted to trash his own home, that was his business and kicking our door. You said not to file charges."

"Thanks Boyd, hire a PI to follow him. I want to know what he's doing and his location, notify me if he leaves town. Keep me updated."

"Will do. Harold was released and that's all I know at this time, but I'll notify you if anything develops."

Gary touched the end button.

Sarah heard the conversation. "Can he find us here?"

"I don't see how. He doesn't know I'm the man, but even if he did, he wouldn't know the location of the ranch. It's very difficult to find, there are a lot of county and private roads that aren't that well marked. Tomorrow, we'll have him located and followed."

She felt better and relaxed. She turned to face him. "Is it time to go to bed? It was a long day. Besides, I need to be held in your arms."

She met his gaze. "Since this will be our home, it's time for us."

He wanted to be sure what she meant. "It's time, what does that mean?"

"For us to become closer. It's time for us to make love. I want to hold my man and become his woman."

He led her down the hallway. "Which bedroom?"

"The one at the end, the big one. I want us to sleep in the big cedar bed under the J brand. I never slept in a bed with a pistol on the bedpost. Should Harold find us, the pistol would be handy. I mean, is it workable?"

"It's workable and loaded. I have mine as well." He pulled up his pants leg and unstrapped an ankle holster and put it on the other bedpost.

Sarah pulled him to the bed and pushed him down in a sitting position and stepped back. She bent and removed her shoes and socks first. Her fingers worked on her shirt and slowly removed it. She tossed it on the dresser and started on the buttons on her jeans. She pushed them down and off and they joined the shirt on the dresser.

His eyes were wide and a smile decorated his lips.

She reached behind and unfastened her bra and tossed it. Next, she shoved the panties off and stood nude in front of him, her arms at her side and her legs slightly open.

She let him look, enjoying the expression on his face and the appreciation gleaming in his eyes.

"How you," she said.

She took his place on the bed and watched him as he watched her undress.

He lifted his shirt and tossed it on the dresser, then loosened his pants and they fell to the floor. He picked them up and put them on the dresser. He slowly worked his underwear down, stepped out, and stood nude in front of her.

"Oh Gary," she whispered as she stood. He pulled her close and she felt his lips on hers in a deep kiss, each savoring the sensation.

Her moans of delight filled the room. After a minute, teasing her with his lips and tongue, he leaned back to see her face and gasped for breath. Her face nuzzled into his chest, enjoying the feel of his hair on her cheeks. She touched his male nipples with the tip of her tongue. He tasted good, and then she worked her way down his muscle harden stomach and was greeted by his hard phallus standing out from his body. Her lips parted in a smile and she leaned forward to kiss the tip.

He placed his hands under her arms and lifted her into his arms. His mouth covered her as he pulled her closer. With his lips still on hers, he lifted her to the bed and followed her down and lay over her.

She loved the feel of his body as he settled in the cradle of her legs. His hard male cylinder, searching for her moist female sheath. His tongue probed deep in her mouth, stroking in the age old rhythm of love. Needing him, she slipped her hand between them and circled his quivering manhood. She shifted him to her damp sex and opened her lips for him.

He shoved forward, feeling her, hot, moist, ready, open. Her legs instinctively moved up his thighs improving the angle of penetration and his thick member stretched her as he entered to the hilt. Her squeal of delight escaped around his lips.

Somewhere deep in her body, her first orgasm started. He released passion she had never experienced before. She thrust up, wanting and demanding more until the intense sensation spread warmly through her body. Her hips went into overdrive as she heaved up against him. Every nerve ending was alive and sending signals of pleasure through her body. He carried her through her first and continued through her second until her legs fell to the bed offering a satisfied sigh.

Only then, did he release her lips and pushed back to see her face. An expression of bliss greeted him. At that moment, he knew. He had truly found his mate for life.

He kissed her face, exploring her nose and eyes. Then down to her chin. She wiggled her breast against the mat of hair on his chest and whispered. "It was wonderful, thank you."

"Thank you. I can't remember ever enjoying it as much as with you."

Suddenly, he sat up. "I didn't use a condom."

"I knew soon after we met that I would be sleeping with you," she said. "I started on the pill."

"I'm glad, it's better the natural way. He began to rise to the occasion again.

She rolled over him and lowered her body down, engulfing him in her moist, warm body. She looked down. "I can't believe I can accommodate you so easily. You're so massive." Her fingers went down and encircle him, feeling his hard member inside her sensitive petals.

His hands cupped her breast and rolled her nipples with his index fingers. She began to rock forward and back, grinding down enjoying the friction on her clitoris. She watched his face, savoring the effect she had on him. His passion quickly reached the pinnacle, her efforts increased to a frenzy of movement on his rigid body, clasping tight, milking him with her female muscles. Her head rolled from side to side, her sandy blond hair dancing with her movements. Her fingers clasped his shoulders, thrusting against him, savoring the delightful sensation as she carried him upward to his moment of bliss.

His muscles tensed and he lifted her from the bed with

his powerful hips. She knew he was nearing his ecstasy.

Out of nowhere, she joined him, surprised, she screamed into her climax. He heaved upward again and again, lifting her from the bed. His hands shifted from her breast to her hips and he pulled and pushed her for their maximum pleasure.

When both were sated, they came down together, and she fell forward on his chest. He met her lips for a kiss, long and loving.

She relaxed and closed her eyes. Satisfied and content, the first time in years. As she kissed him, tears of joy and happiness filtered through her senses. His arms slid around her waist, holding her tight, but not uncomfortable, just right. Everything between them perfect.

Sometime later, he rolled her to his side. She woke from her nap and happily kissed his cheek. His lips brushed her lips,

Her eyes went to his and saw only gentleness. "Was it as good for you as it was for me?" she asked.

"Never have I enjoyed it as much," he said. "I've never felt more wanted and needed. We need to sleep for a while, then we're going to talk and make love again."

"Talk about what?" she asked as a hint of worry wrinkled her forehead.

"Us, your divorce and getting married."

"Please give me time before asking me. You'll know when the moment is right and I'll say, yes."

She found his shoulder and was asleep in seconds.

She woke in his arms and kissed his cheeks until he opened his eyes. "I'll make breakfast for us. My first meal to cook for you here."

Sarah slid from the bed and went to her bags for a robe. He patted her bare bottom as he passed on the way to the bathroom.

She found eggs and bacon and made toast. A pot of coffee was brewing when he came to the kitchen and pulled her into his arms for a good morning kiss.

They ate on the deck overlooking the pond and watched ducks as they flew into the morning sunlight.

"I have the men plant a field of corn for the wild birds. Of course deer and turkey go there as well."

She saw movement in the trees surrounding the pond. Two does with fawns came to the water to drink.

"There is usually a trophy buck with them," he said. A few moments passed before the massive deer stepped from the brush and followed the does to the water, but kept looking around and raising his head to test the air for possible danger.

"He's so majestic," she exclaimed. "Like you. I can sense your importance, like the buck. I can picture you here on the ranch more than I can in a boardroom."

"I enjoy both. When I'm here, this is where I belong, but when I'm in the boardroom, I also feel that is where I belong. I'm fortunate to have the best of both worlds and the right woman with me."

His hand slid over and covered hers.

They finished eating in silence, watching the pond. "Let's dress and I'll start the tour," he suggested. "I want you to meet Juan and Maria. The cowboys will be gone by now."

They dressed in jeans and shirts. He pulled on his ranch boots with spurs on them. "You need riding boots," he said.

***

Maria came to the door at his knock. She saw Gary and Sarah. "Mister Gary, welcome. So this is Sarah?"

"This is Sarah. The woman of my dreams and the woman I'm going to marry. Meet Sarah." The two woman took the others hand and they smiled.

He explained how Maria knew about her. "I talk to Juan almost every day. He keeps me informed on what's going on here. I told him about you and you would be coming with me."

Maria stepped back and invited them inside. "Juan is at the barn doing something. I heard him mention there was something broken in one of the stalls."

She led Sarah to the table. "I have coffee and cookies."

"I'll have to take a rain check," she said. "We had breakfast only a few minutes ago. I'm staying when Gary goes back to work and I would love to have coffee and cookies with you. I want time to get acquainted."

She glanced at Gary, then back at Maria. "He said I would be staying here for a while, he mentioned something like seventy years."

Maria beamed. "Juan has said Mister Gary would never bring a woman here. I said the right woman would come along sooner or later and he would bring her home. I was right."

They visited for a few minutes before Gary stood. "I'm giving her a tour of the ranch. We'll go to the barn and she can meet Juan."

"Do you want me to cook something for you today?" Maria asked.

"Thanks," Sarah said, "but that's my job now." She circled his waist with her arm. "I want to cook for my man."

Maria smiled. "I understand, but if you need anything give me a call."

They found Juan putting a new board on one of the stalls. He saw them come through the door, stopped working, and wiped his brow with his sleeve. He then removed gloves and met them and shook hands with Gary. "Welcome home, Mr. Justice."

"It's good to be here and this is Sarah."

She stuck out her hand to shake. "It's nice to meet you Juan. We met Maria a few minutes ago."

They walked outside to catch the breeze. It was hot inside the barn. Gary began discussing the ranch. Sarah listened to the talk and realized there was a lot she needed to learn. What they were discussing was foreign to her. She saw two horses in the corral. One was a golden brown with a lighter mane and tail. She walked to the fence and the pretty horse came to the fence to be petted. Sarah climbed up on the fence and petted the horse on the nose and neck.

Gary came to the fence. "This is April. She was named April because she was born on April 1st, five years ago. She's gentle and well mannered."

"Hello, April." The horse was nudging Sarah's hand. "She expects something to eat," Gary explained. "Like an apple or cookie. I'm afraid she's spoiled, a real pet. From now on, bring her food when you come here."

"I will. She's beautiful."

"I hoped you would like her, she's yours now."

"Mine," Sarah exclaimed. "You mean, like for me to ride? I've ridden some, but I'm not an accomplished horsewoman."

"You'll learn and now is a good time to start. Juan, will you bring them into the barn."

Gary led Sarah to the tack room and pulled a bridle and saddle from a rack. I think this is your size."

She wanted to ask about the saddle, but held back and walked to where Juan led the two horses. Gary took his and began to brush his back. Juan picked up a brush and started on April's back. "Can I do it," Sarah asked, "but please tell me what to do."

Juan handed the brush to Sarah and watched as she worked brushing the dirt from the mare's back from rolling in the corral. When she finished, he handed her the blanket and then the saddle. He helped her lift it and instructed her how to cinch it tight.

Gary had his gelding saddled and led him to Sarah and April. The horses followed them out of the barn and Gary offered his hand to help Sarah on the saddle. April stood still, waiting for her rider to get settled. Gary put his foot in the stirrup and swung up on his horse.

Maria came out of the house with two sacks. "You may get hungry before you get back. She handed one to Sarah. "I put several extra cookies in your sack in case you need them for April."

Sarah thanked her and saw Gary putting his sack in his saddlebag and she did the same.

Juan and Maria watched them ride away. They were smiling and holding hands, happy Gary had found his woman.

"I can't wait for children," Maria sighed. "It's been so long since I heard the sound of children laughing and playing."

They rode slowly, letting Sarah become comfortable.

April was a good horse and well trained. She seemed to understand her rider was inexperienced and did her best to help.

Gary found his two cowboys working on a windmill and introduced Sarah. Brock and Sam were their names. Sarah judged they were both in their late forties or early fifties. Both looked like cowboys. Lean, tan and their faces reflected a life outside in the elements.

Brock walked to April and patted her on the nose. "Sorry gal, I'm fresh out of cookies. Jane Ann always fed you and I know you expect a cookie."

Sarah reached back and opened her saddlebag and found a cookie and handed it to Brock. He broke it into four pieces and gave one piece to the horse. As they talked, Brock fed the horse the other three pieces.

When they rode away, she had to ask. "Who was Jane Ann? Did April belong to her? What happened to her?"

Gary grinned at her questions, he knew she was curious. She knew that the horse didn't belong to his wife. Her name was Connie, so who was Jane Ann.

"Jane Ann is his daughter. She trained April to be a cow horse and worked cattle with her dad. She married a rancher and moved to Montana. I bought her for you and the saddle. They needed the money to buy breeding stock for their ranch."

"Why did you buy her for me? I mean, couldn't she be used as a working horse for Brock or Sam?"

"They wouldn't ride her; she's too small for them. Besides I furnish them horses."

"You evaded my question," she said.

"I know. But since you asked, I bought her for you when I decided I was going to bring you home and be my wife. That is, when you agree."

Sarah rode for a few minutes, thinking. "When did you buy her?"

"I think it was the week after the picnic. Why did you want to know when?"

"Curiosity I suppose. How did you know I would be visiting the ranch and would enjoy having a horse to ride?"

"An easy enough question. I knew then I wanted you and intended to bring you here someday. That is, if you felt the same and wanted to come with me."

Sarah patted April on the neck and enjoyed the emotion Gary had installed inside her chest. He always said the right things.

They spent time riding and she enjoyed seeing the ranch. At noon, he led her to a grove of pecan trees and stepped down from his horse and helped her. A small spring-fed stream ran through the valley and the grass was lush and the trees majestic. The two horses were tied with his rope and allowed to graze. They opened the sacks and ate roast beef sandwiches.

It was almost sunset when they entered the corral. Before they dismounted, they sat in the saddle and watched the sun slip behind the ridge in the west.

Juan was there to meet them and took the reins from Sarah. Gary came over and helped her down. She moaned in pain. Her thighs and back hurt. She knew she would be sore, but it was worth it. It had been a wonderful outing with Gary.

She gave April the last cookie, and then helped Juan brush her horse and give her hay and oats according to Juan's instruction. As they left the barn, Maria met them at the door to the house. "I know you said you would cook for Mr. Gary, but I knew you wouldn't be home in time and after riding so much, you might not feel like cooking. Your supper is in the oven."

Sarah thanked her. "You're right." She rubbed the back of her thighs and butt.

"Soaking in a hot bath will help," Maria offered.

Gary followed her inside and closed the door. "Go ahead and get in the tub. I'll mix a drink and bring it to you."

He found her in almost steaming hot water. She smiled when he entered. "The hot water hurt a few places when I first got in, but it feels good now. I may have a couple of raw spots from the way it stings."

"I have lotion and liniment and will doctor you when you get out. It'll take time riding before can you do it

105

without hurting. In fact, I feel a few sore spots as well."

She reached for the drink he offered and took a long swallow and put the glass on the side of the tub. She patted the water. "There's room for two."

He hurried to undress and slid in with her. She gave him room to move behind her and lay back against his chest. His arms circled her and rubbed her shoulders and arms.

When the water cooled, she stepped out first and reached for a towel. He followed and picked up another. She wrapped the towel around her body and went to the bedroom.

He opened the door of the medicine cabinet and took out two bottles and followed her. She sat on the bed, waiting for him. He reached for her towel and she rolled on her stomach. He groaned. "You said a couple of raw spots. Sarah you have two saddle sores on your butt. Those had to be hurting like the devil before we got home. Why didn't you tell me?"

"We were horseback and the only way to get home was ride or walk and I chose riding even thought it hurt."

He went back to the bathroom and came back with a tube of ointment and two large band-aids. He put a dollop on the gauze and placed it over the raw places. She grimaced and groaned.

"I know it hurts, but the salve will help. I use it on a regular basis. A doctor prescribed it for me for scrapes and cuts."

He rubbed her back and thighs with the liniment, then the rest of her body with lotion.

Gary stepped back and enjoyed her body. She slid from the bed and stood. Her eyes slid down and she reached for him. "Down big boy. I'm starved and with my sore spots and aching legs, we may have to wait until I feel better. Besides, it's your fault; you took me on that long ride."

He lifted her in his arms and kissed her lips. "We'll see later, but you're right, I'm hungry as hell."

They found steak and all the usual vegetables common in ranch cooking. A peach pie was also in the oven. Sarah ate like a field hand. "Bless Maria," she said. "I wouldn't have had time or the energy to cook for you tonight."

He took her hands and lifted her from the chair. "Go on and get ready for bed. I'll take care of the kitchen." He put the dishes in the sink and the food in the refrigerator and went to the bedroom. She was pulling the cover down. The only thing she was wearing was the two band-aids.

He undressed and she saw the pistol on his leg. She glanced at the bedpost. "I didn't know you took it with you today, why?"

"As a precaution, for snakes, coyotes, varmints."

"And Harold," she added.

"I doubt he would come here, he doesn't know about us, as yet, but there are ways he may find out. Everybody at the bank knows. The police know. There was no need taking chances of being found unarmed. Besides, I always carry a pistol here. Brock and Sam had weapons in their truck, which is the way it is here."

He joined her on the bed and pulled up the cover. She rolled to him and put her head on his shoulder. "Would you be disappointed if we don't make love tonight? My butt and legs are sore."

He caressed her cheeks and neck. "Since you mentioned it, I think I need a good night's sleep. We'll have plenty to time. Remember, we have our seventy years."

She kissed him and relaxed. She could never remember being as happy and contented. She had found her home, finally.

They were asleep in a matter of minutes.

Chapter 10

Harold Nance wanted to run, but kept his cool when the policeman stopped him for running the light. He expected to be arrested, but he was issued a citation and released on his own recognizance. He decided to go home instead of finding a bar. He had plans to make.

Besides following Gary Justice was a bad idea anyway. He let his temper get the best of him and retaliation against him would cause more problems than bashing in his face with his fist.

Besides, Gary seemed fit and well muscled; he might get his face smashed if he picked a fight.

***

Harold woke early and called a cleaning service and made arrangements for his house to be cleaned. There was nothing to eat, so he went to the car and drove to a fast food place and bought a couple of breakfast biscuits and a large coffee.

The list of possible men that Sarah was with was in his pocket. The first, the school principal, Billy Swan. He had looked up the addresses in the phone book.

He parked in front of a house three doors down from Swan's home and sat back to wait and read the paper. It was over an hour before the garage door opened and a car backed out with a woman on the passenger side.

Her face wasn't clear enough for him to see if it was Sarah. He started the car and followed a half block behind the gray car. If it was Sarah, she might be cautious and look behind and would recognize his car.

The gray car turned into a food store and parked. Harold grabbed his binoculars and focused on the woman as she got out. His heart raced for a moment, she had the same physical appearance as Sarah, but when she turned toward his car, he saw it wasn't Sarah.

The man joined her and they went into the store holding hands. Harold cursed and marked Swan from his list.

The next name, Norman Wagner, the physical education teacher. The address was in the same area of town.

This time, he didn't have to wait. A man he recognized as Wagner was mowing grass. Harold stopped and waited. The man finished mowing and took the mower to the garage. The door was up. Another man came out of the house and met Wagner. However, the man was dressed as a woman. They kissed and put their arms around the other and went back into the house and the door went down. Nausea caused Harold to gag. How any man could kiss another man was beyond him.

He scratched Wagner from his list so hard he tore the paper.

The next name, Carl Benton, but called Bud. A teacher at the same school with Sarah. He wasn't familiar with the address and opened a city map he brought along. The address was on the opposite side of town. The older side, near the railroad.

It took him over thirty minutes to find the house. It was a fifties home, though neat with a fresh coat of paint. It stood out in the dilapidated neighborhood.

As a precaution, he locked his car doors and placed his pistol on the seat. Several men passed and he suspected if the car had been vacant, his tires and anything else that could be removed would be gone. Two men stopped and eyed him and the car. He placed the weapon on the dash and the two men made a hasty retreat.

It was mid afternoon before the door opened. An elderly woman came outside followed by a younger man. They walked to a nearby deli and bought something. They returned to the house and went inside.

Harold wasn't sure enough to scratch Bud from the list. He went to counter at the deli and bought a sandwich. "Who was that elderly woman with a younger man?" he casually asked. "They looked familiar, but I can't recall his name."

"That was Irma and Bud Benton," the helpful lady replied. "He teaches school and lives with his mother. They walk here almost every day for her exercise. He's such a devoted young man, but I feel sorry for him. He never goes out, and has never dated, well that I know about and I've worked here for ten years. When his mother dies, I often wonder what he'll do."

Harold again cursed as he sat in his car and ate the sandwich. His mouth watered for a beer, but again he pushed that thought back in the recesses of his mind.

However, the thought of a cold brew kept surfacing with each bit of the sandwich. Finally, the urge overruled his common sense. He started the car and drove until he found a package store and bought a six pack.

The first, he drank without taking a breath. The second, he downed half and took a breath and finished the remainder. On the third, he took two swallows and placed the bottle in the holder and started the car. He drank the remaining beer on the drive across town.

He finished the last beer and stopped and bought a liter of liquor and two quarts of beer. Wanting a drink of the whisky caused him to rush home. He took a large swallow and sat in his recliner. Harold took another swallow of the booze and chased it with beer.

He knew he should never have bought the six pack. Once he tasted the beer, he couldn't stop.

Harold tossed the two lids toward the trash can and missed. He shrugged, what the hell, the cleaning people will be here.

The familiar feeling of bliss settled into his body as the alcohol took effect. He reached for the phone book and opened the top page and found the list of frequently used numbers Sarah had entered. Tommy Hall was listed. He grinned. Why had Sarah kept bringing the number forward from year to year?

He dialed. A woman answered. Harold knew it wasn't Sarah's voice. "Is Tommy there?" he asked.

"Just a moment, I'll get him," the woman said.

He recognized Tommy's voice when he answered.

"This is Harold Nance."

A silence greeted him for a long moment. "What the hell do you want and why are you calling me?" Tommy shouted.

Harold was ready with a reply. "I made a mistake, and I wanted to apologize."

"It's too late for that ass hole. You burned that bridge, so fuck off Nance."

"Just a moment, I want to ask you something. Sarah left me for another man. I want to know who. Did she ever mention anybody?"

"No shit. It wasn't me, and that was the reason you called. You suspected it was me. I'm happily married to Jennifer, and I haven't seen or talked to Sarah since that day. I don't blame her for leaving your sorry ass. You're nothing but a stupid drunk. If you show up at my home or give Jennifer or me any trouble you'll be a dead drunk. And don't call again, ever."

Tommy slammed the phone down.

He wasn't convinced, so he didn't mark Tommy Hall from his list.

He took another long pull from the liquor bottle and finished off one of the quarts of beer. He would choose three more names from the list tomorrow.

He woke when somebody rang the doorbell. He got out of his recliner where he slept and went to the door. It was the cleaning service. He invited them in and pointed. "Start with the den and kitchen. Throw anything away that you feel isn't good or needed. Put everything else where it belongs."

The two women went to work and Harold went to the bathroom. He showered and shaved and put on fresh clothes. He left the women and went to his car and drove to a café and ate a hardy breakfast. That made him feel better.

What to do next? He drank another cup of coffee and selected the next three names on his list, but had little hope. They were all long shots anyway, but he needed to check them out.

The first was Howard Thomas, a classmate of Sarah in college. He recalled Howard as being wimpy, but Sarah liked him, and had a few dates before Harold.

He located Howard's home and waited across the street. He was shocked when a nurse pushed Howard out in a wheelchair. The nurse loaded Howard in a van with a lift. Harold followed them to a physical therapy clinic and followed them inside. An attendant met Howard and pushed him away to a room. The nurse sat in chair to wait. Harold sat beside her. "Wasn't that Howard Thomas you brought in?" he asked.

"Yes," she replied.

"What happened to him?" he asked.

"Car wreck about a month ago. Both legs are paralyzed. We hope therapy will help, but I have my doubts he'll ever walk again."

"I'm sorry," he mumbled and walked away, leaving the nurse wondering.

The next on his list was Manuel Lopez. He had never seen or met the man, but Sarah talked about him and said he was a nice guy. Sarah met Manny doing volunteer work during the summer. They worked together on a fundraiser for meals on wheels and delivered meals to the elderly several times.

He found Manny and was dumfounded. Manny was grossly overweight. He was also nearing sixty. Harold scratched him off the list immediately.

The last on his list was Monty Bilberry. Sarah hired Monty to do yard work and paint the trim on the house. Every summer, Monty came to the house to mow and did any repair work needed on the house.

There was nobody and home. He saw a neighbor across the street from Monty's home and walked over to ask. The neighbor said, "Monty is a hard worker. He leaves early and come home late."

"What about his wife," Harold asked.

"She works at Wal-Mart and works as hard as Monty. I admire them; they have it all tighter and are a happily married couple."

Harold went to his car and scratched Monty from the list. Harold drove home in thought.

The men he had on his list was proving a waste of time, but he had to find her and the man she was shacking with.

He sat in his recliner and opened a beer. "Who would know?" he toward the bottle. "Somebody that Sarah might confide with."

He almost spilled his beer. Abby Bagwell, of course, Sarah's friend from school. They often talked on the phone. If anybody knew, it would be Abby. From Sarah's comments, Abby was inquisitive and a gossip. If there was any juicy scandal around school, surely Abby would know.

He decided to find Abby, but after drinking beer, he needed to eat. He stopped for a burger and fries. The waitress came to his table and left his ticket. He pulled out a ten and handed it to her. "Keep the change," he said. She frowned, what a tipper, less than a dollar tip.

"Do you have a phone book?" He forgot to bring theirs from home. She went to the front and brought back the book and handed it to him.

He searched and found several Bagwell's listed. He ripped out the page and tossed the book on the table and walked out. The waitress gestured at his back with her middle finger.

There were twenty-two Bagwell's, but none were listed as Abby, but that didn't mean anything. The name could be in her husband's name or not listed. There were two with the initials A.

Harold dialed the first and asked for Abby. "Wrong number buddy," a man said, gruffly. "There's nobody here by that name."

The second call, a woman answered. "Abby," he said.

"This is Alice," she purred. "Could I help you with anything?"

That startled Nance. "How can you help me? I mean, what do you do?" he asked.

"If you don't know, forget it." The phone went dead.

Using the addresses for Bagwell's from the phone book, he made a list of the orders to call. The odds were Abby lived near the school.

Harold wished for a drink, but pushed that thought to

the back of his mind and started calling. Out of the first ten, no answers on six and four was negative.

The next ten proved to be worse. Seven no answers and three negatives. Thirteen were left to call.

A thought popped into his mind. He hit his head as a gesture of not thinking of it sooner. Sarah had a directory of the faculty in her desk. He hurried home and found the floor spotless around the desk. The cleaning ladies had already picked up the papers. He searched the stack of papers they placed on the desk. It wasn't there and the cleaning people were gone. He had pulled everything out of the desk drawers searching for his car keys and tossed it on the floor. The cleaning ladies threw almost everything away.

He went to the back fence and found four plastic bags of trash in the alley. He wasn't about to go through them in search of the directory. Spoiled food was in the bags.

Harold went back into the house and found the den clean and the beer and liquor bottles were gone. He doubted there was any left anyway. He rarely left any in a bottle.

He picked up his phone and found Sarah's name and called. A message advised him the phone was not in service. He suspected she had it turned off.

He searched his brain, thinking, who could she be with? Did they have sex last night? Of course they did. Sarah was an attractive woman and most men would welcome her to his bed, even if she was a dud in the sack. She was sleeping with the bastard. If he only knew who.

One consolation. Sarah wasn't passionate. She didn't say no, but then she wasn't responsive. Making love to her was never exciting and of late, it wasn't worth the effort. He found more satisfaction in a bottle than her body.

The thought of the effect alcohol had was more than he could stand. He went to the car and rushed to the liquor store and bought a liter and a fifth of liquor and four quarts of beer.

He downed half of one of the quarts on the way home. Harold was so intense in finding Sarah, he never thought of anybody spying on him.

A white car had tailed him. He wasn't aware a man

came into the café where he ate. Or had opened the phone book for the page number Harold tore out.

The private detective called Gary and reported Harold was searching for somebody whose name began with B. "Abby Bagwell," Sarah said. "She's my friend. Harold wants to find her and see if she knows where I am and who I'm with. She knows about you, I'm sure of it. She saw us at the school."

She opened her purse and found her address book and gave Garry Abby's address and phone number. He gave it to the detective and requested her home be under surveillance should Harold go there.

Sarah was worried about her friend. Gary noticed and said, "Call Abby and tell her that Harold is searching for you. She needs to know and can be cautious."

Abby's home phone didn't answer. Sarah called her cell phone. Abby answered and Sarah explained what had happened. "Harold is looking for you. I'm sure he wants to ask you who I'm with, and where I am. He's dangerous. He wants to kill me."

Abby was calmer than Sarah suspected. "Harold will have a hell of a time finding me. I'm visiting an aunt in New Mexico. I'll be here for at least two months. My aunt is in poor health and I'm caring for her this summer."

That was a relief. "Is there any way Harold could get your address in New Mexico?"

"No way. We're at a resort. We selected it after I got here. Nobody knows where I am and I'll keep it that way."

"You managed to evade me at school," Abby said. "And I haven't forgiven you for that. Since you're obligated to me now, tell me. How good is Gary?"

Sarah smiled, now that school was out and she wouldn't be back in the fall, she decided to reply. "On a scale of one to ten, he's at least a fifteen and possible sixteen."

Abby giggled. "Is he well endowed, and does he have staying power?"

"Your impossible," Sarah giggled. "You know that, but he's everything I ever dreamed about and staying power. I guess I can answer that by saying, I'm riding horseback every

115

day and Gary is riding me every night.

Abby offered a big sigh. "I envy you. Are you still in town?"

"Of course not. Gary took me to a rustic house, far away. It's beautiful here. The mountains are majestic, and I can see snow on the peaks. The streams are full of trout and there's abundant wild life, elk, moose and deer. I may have seen a bear today, but he was hidden in the trees."

He's taking me across the border tomorrow. I've never been out of the United States and I'm looking forward to it."

"As I said, there's a horse for me to ride and I have two strawberry-like saddle sores on my butt, and my thighs are so sore I can hardly walk."

"What does Gary say about that? I mean, being sore?"

"He's gentle and understands and is doctoring my hurts."

She changed the subject. Should Harold find you, tell him what I said. It'll help throw him off my trail. I don't want him badgering my friends."

She decided to tease Abby a little as a payback for the times she had badgered her for details.

"Oh my God, stop doing that," she moaned. "I'm on the phone with my friend Abby. Don't you ever get enough?" She paused for effect, and then added more. "Oh, you feel so good." She gave a mighty squeal and sigh just before she touched the end button. Then she turned the phone off. She suspected Abby would call back immediately.

Gary was laughing. "A devious side of my fair Sarah I didn't know about. The more I learn about you, the more I love you. You handled that like a champ. Your quick witted and sharp. Thinking on your feet is a wonderful trait. That last part was a stroke of genius and it turned me on. I wonder if it frustrated Abby."

Sarah smiled as she glanced below Gary's belt buckle.

"Abby will be convinced we're near Canada," he said. "Trout, elk, moose, and bear aren't found in the arid southwest. I doubt there has been a black bear seen here in a hundred years, if ever."

Gary called the detective agency and cancelled the surveillance on Abby's home.

He wanted to pat her on her butt, but held back. "How do the saddle sores feel?"

"Not bad, but I can definitely feel them. My thighs are better, much better."

"I think I need to check the bandages and put on more medicine."

She helped him with her clothing before rolling on her hands and knees on the bed. He pulled the band-aids from the sore places and found them healing nicely. He replaced the bandages with fresh salve.

Sarah glanced over her shoulder. Teasing Abby also had an effect on her. "I never did it this way."

He jerked his pants and shorts off and got on his knees and put his hands on her hips and she reached between her legs and positioned him. He entered her slowly and enjoyed her sigh of pleasure. With care, he lay over her and caressed her breast with his hands. She was now thrusting back to meet him and making sexy sounds each time he entered her to the hilt. She began to chant as her passion increased. "Faster, harder, so good, yes, I love this," she gasped. "I'm getting close, now, now, yes. Oh God, Gary, I love you."

He felt her body go rigid and slammed into her with all his strength. She grabbed the bedspread with her hands to keep him from pushing her into the headboard. The experience was unbelievable, and she responded with wild passion as her time of bless reached the crest. His body responded and he filled her with his love.

She fell forward on her face and he went down over her, but held his weight with his knees and elbows. She moaned her pleasure and relaxed. He moved to her side and held her in his arms.

He leaned close and kissed her lips. "Each time gets better. Did I hurt your sore places?"

"What sore places?" she joked. "I loved it that way. But then I haven't found a position I didn't enjoy with you."

***

Harold settled into the recliner and tuned the television

117

on and started sipping the hard liquor. The warmth spread through his body and he relaxed. If he could find Sarah and the man she left him for, he would dispose of them, sell the house and move to Mexico. With the money he had from the bank and the sale of the house, he could live in leisure. It should be easy to hire a maid to take care of the house and he could lie on a warm beach and drink cold beer. Liquor sells for a third of the cost in the states. Should the need of female company be needed, that would be available on demand.

It was almost noon when Harold woke and stumbled to the bathroom. A shower helped, but he needed coffee. He made instant and drank two cups before he felt like dressing. An egg and sausage biscuit at a drive through helped.

He needed help locating Abby's home. Not knowing her address, it could take forever to locate her. The only way he could find her would be to ring the bell on each or watch houses for her. That could take forever.

He decided to try the school where Sarah and Abby taught. He suspected the school building would be empty, but he was lucky, he saw a man painting. Harold talked to him and learned he worked for a contractor that had a contract to paint the school. He advised his wife was a teacher and he came for a few of her things from her room.

The worker seemed indifferent. Harold went inside and hurried to Abby's room. He started with her desk and it took only a few minutes to locate a receipt from a store with Abby's address.

The painter was mixing paint at his truck when Harold left. He didn't speak when Harold went to his car. Abby's home wasn't far from the school.

He was disappointed when he stopped in front of a small frame home. It looked deserted, but he needed to check. He rang the bell several times and peeked in the window. It was dark and had the appearance of being closed for the summer. There wasn't a car in the garage and the gate to the backyard was locked.

Dejected, he walked toward his car when a neighbor spoke. "May I help you with something?"

"I hope so? I'm looking for Abby Bagwell."

"She's not here. She left the morning after school dismissed for the summer. She's visiting an aunt in New Mexico. She said she would be gone for two months, or until just before school starts this fall."

"I see. Would you have her phone number? It's important I talk with her."

"Who are you?" The woman asked.

"Harold Nance. I'm Sarah's husband. They are friends."

The woman began backing away. It was obvious she was suddenly frightened. "Abby told me about you. If you don't leave immediately, I'm calling the cops." She turned and ran for the safety of her home.

That was all he needed, another encounter with the police. He hurried to his car and drove away. Information from Abby was now out of the question, even if he could locate her. If she told her neighbor about him, then she certainly wouldn't give him information. That is, except under force. That thought pleased him since he never liked Abby. She continually made snide remarks about him and looked down on him as if he was a homeless drunken bum.

The bank came to mind as an option, but it was closed. He saw a liquor store and decided he needed to supplement his supply. He wasn't sure how much remained. He bought two liters and a three case of beer in quart bottles.

He couldn't think of anything he could do to locate Sarah and the man she left with, other than back to his original list. His anger flared and he slammed his fist on the wheel in front of him as he drove home.

A police car turned and followed him. He drove carefully and sighed when he turned into his drive and opened his garage door with the remote. The police car stopped in front of his house and Harold turned and saw the cop talking on his radio as the garage door closed. A white car passed, but he didn't notice it as his vision was on the policeman. He wondered if the busy-body neighbor of Abby called the police. Or maybe they were keeping tabs on him after the incidents.

He glanced down at the booze and was glad he wasn't stopped. He suspected the law had him targeted and would make it hard on him if he was stopped. He also had his weapons in the car. He shivered at the thought of what they would have done if those were found.

Harold opened the car door, but before he got out, he opened a bottle of liquor and guzzled several swallows and gasped as he opened a beer to chase it. The alcohol eased his tension and he carried the bottles inside the house. He found he had the fifth of liquor, and about a half quart of beer. He was happy he bought more. Being out scared him.

***

Abby's neighbor, Nancy, called the police and reported Harold Nance was at Abby's home and explained the significance. The policeman assured Nancy they would send a car, but unless Nance broke the law, there was nothing they could do. Nancy called Abby on her cell phone. "Harold Nance was at your home looking for you. I didn't tell him a thing; well I told him you were in New Mexico. I didn't know who he was until after I mentioned that. I reported him to the police."

"It's fine," Abby replied. "He's trying to find Sarah. He threatened to kill her. I talked to her earlier and she's somewhere up north. I think near Canada at a resort. I'm glad Harold can't find her." Abby stopped short of giving more details.

"As I said, I called the cops and told them about Harold prowling around your house. They're checking on him."

"Thanks, Harold is bad news and I'm glad Sarah left him. He needs to be committed or put in jail before he hurts somebody. I'm convinced if he finds Sarah, he would kill her. If he comes back, but I doubt he will since he knows I'm not there. But if he does, call the cops immediately and lock your doors. That man is crazy."

***

Gary held Sarah in his arms. "Want to dress and drive into town for dinner tonight?"

"I will if that's want you want?"

"What had you rather do?" he asked.

She rolled over and put her head on his chest. "I had rather cook a meal for my man. Mix us a cocktail, and sit in front of the fireplace, or on the deck and enjoy being alone with you. I'm loving being here and relaxing. It's been hectic for the past several days, or I should have said, weeks. In fact, I haven't been this comfortable in years. Later, I want to come back to our bed and make love. If you don't mind, we can go into town later. This is the first time since I married Harold I feel comfortable with love. It's like I've come home after a long absence and this is where I belong."

She turned her head and saw his misty eyes. His hands were trembling as they stroked her back and shoulders. She never felt so loved and wanted as she did at this moment. Gary had evolved into being her life. Without him, she knew she would be nothing, but with him, she was everything.

Chapter 11

Harold started on the booze without eating and soon was almost in a stupor. He knew he should quit drinking, but he opened another quart of beer and poured a generous amount down his throat. He put the bottle on the table and slumped back in the chair and passed out.

It was Monday afternoon before he came back from his alcoholic stupor. Every time he woke, he would pull on the bottles and go to sleep. Shaking his head to clear the cobwebs, he made it to the bathroom and into the shower. It helped some, but he needed food. He hadn't eaten since he couldn't remember when.

Aspirin would help. With a gulp of water, he swallowed four and went to the kitchen. There was nothing in the refrigerator. His hands shook so bad he spilled the coffee and dropped the glass he used to pour water into the pot.

In disgust, he found pants and shirt on the floor of his closet. The alcohol was still in command of his mind, but he stumbled to the car and drove to a fast food place for coffee and two breakfast burritos. That helped and he drove home.

There was a white car behind him, but he didn't notice.

The PI recorded the trip in his notebook and parked in the shade of a tree. His orders weren't to report to Justice unless something significant happened.

Harold shaved and found jeans and a clean shirt in the closet. The food and aspirin helped and his determination to find Sarah and her lover gave him the strength to go out.

There were still names on his original list. He selected three more and began locating their addresses. First was John Settle, her high school boyfriend. The next was a Bobby Butler, a man that had lived next door two or three years ago. Bobby and Maxine were friends of Sarah until she died. Bobby sold the house and moved, but who knows, maybe Sarah and Bobby met after that.

The next was Clarence McMeans, a single parent. Sarah helped tutor his child. She often invited the little girl to their home and Clarence brought her and sometimes waited while Sarah worked with the child.

He found a John Settle in the phone book and called. A woman answered and he knew it wasn't Sarah. The woman talked with an English accent. He hung up.

Harold found two Bobby Butlers in the phone book. Neither answered when he called. He moved on to Clarence McMeans. He found his name and called. A woman answered, he wasn't sure, so in a disguised tone, he asked for Clarence McMeans. The woman asked, "Who is calling?" Harold decided to lie. "George, an old friend from long ago. I'm in town and decided to give Clarence a call."

"Clarence died two months ago," the woman said. "I'm sorry," Harold said and hung up.

That left only Bobby Butler on his list.

He felt better now and drove to the address of the first Butler listed in the phone book.

The house looked as if nobody lived there. Grass and weeds were in the yard. He noticed a sign and walked to it. It was a, for sale sign. He dialed the number and inquired about the house. The realtor was very helpful. She said, "That property has been vacant for over six months. Mr. Butler was transferred in his job. He and his wife moved to Boston."

Harold thanked her and drove to the home of the second Butler. He waited across the street and saw a man and woman drive out of the garage. They were both black.

He cursed as he marked Bobby Butler from his list. There might be more Butler's, but they weren't in the phone book. Besides that was a remote possibility and he had the gut feeling he wasn't the man with Sarah.

Harold knew these were all long-shots, but he had no other choices that came to mind.

He drove home and walked in and sat on the couch.

As he sat, thinking, he noticed something wrong. Something was missing. Then it dawned on him, the china

123

hutch that belonged to her grandmother was gone.

With a string of curse words, he hurried to her bedroom. An empty closet greeted him. Also, her special bedspread was gone and everything of hers from the bathroom was missing.

Dejected, he went back to the bar and began to think. The only time she could have moved her things was on Friday. School always ends at noon on the last day. She moved during the afternoon while he was at the bank.

Thinking back, Justice didn't call him to his office until four. He wondered at the time why it took so long. Somebody was giving Sarah time to move. She couldn't have done it alone in that length of time, and somebody with a truck or trailer had to move the hutch. It was packed with china, and was much too large and heavy for her to move alone.

Somebody at the bank was in on it. Boyd, Young or Justice. Then it hit him, Marvin drove a pickup. It was all coming together in his mind.

Boyd and Young were much too old for her, and Marvin was early twenties. He was a recent college graduate. His mind ran through the men employees of the bank. None seemed to be a viable candidate as her lover. That left Gary Justice. But how? She didn't know him. And then he remembered the picnic. She said Justice and Marvin helped her.

"Sarah left me for my boss," he shouted. He knew Gary had an apartment in town, but owned a ranch, somewhere west. Harold had no idea where it was located.

It all fit now, Marvin helped Sarah move while Justice kept him at the bank delaying the meeting to give them time. She had been sleeping with him at his apartment, and was there or at the ranch with him. The ranch was more logical with the long weekend.

She was waiting for him at his apartment. If the cop hadn't stopped him running the light, he would have followed Justice that Friday afternoon, and caught them together.

He tossed the names he had written in the trash and

picked up the scratch pad and in bold letters, wrote, Gary Justice. Then under it, he wrote, Sarah Nance. He placed a large X over their names.

What did Justice see in Sarah? He wondered. She's far from being a beauty, she wasn't passionate, and didn't have money. What did she have to offer a handsome man like Gary with more money than God? He could almost pick any woman he wanted. Had he missed something in Sarah?

"No matter," he said to himself. "They'll share a common grave when I find them."

***

Sarah and Gary relaxed and enjoyed their time talking; allowing her saddle sores time to heal and the soreness leave her thighs. With each passing hour, Gary was more and more convinced Sarah was perfect in everything he wanted in a woman and wife. Her personality, her features, her attitude, and openness appealed to him. She was beautiful in his eyes and intelligent and educated. A teacher, and would be a super mother to their children. She scored a perfect 10 in his mind.

She felt the same about Gary. She had never been this happy and contented. He opened a new door in her life that she didn't know existed. She had dreamed of the knight in shining armor that would ride into her world and scoop her up and carry her away to his kingdom.

The ranch wasn't a kingdom, and Gary wasn't a knight, but the ranch and Gary in his faded jeans and boots were damn close. She leaned over and kissed his sweet lips and purred like a contented kitten.

If only that bastard Harold wasn't in the picture, their life would be paradise. They both knew at some point in the their future, he must be dealt with. Gary would be forced to go back into town and be at the bank each morning. Harold could easily find Gary's apartment or target him any morning as he left for work.

A cold shiver ran down her spine at those horrid thoughts. It wouldn't be fair if Harold killed or injured Gary because of her.

125

Chapter 12

Harold had to be positive before he made his next move. It was easy to find the address of Gary Justice. He glanced at the clock. He would wait until midnight before going after them.

A cold beer helped sooth his keyed up nerves as she waited.

He checked his pistol and put it in a holster on his back, under his shirt, but where he could reach it with ease.

He put the rifle in the back seat and covered it with a blanket. He wanted to be ready when he found them.

The PI was parked at the end of the street and saw Harold leave his garage. He waited and made a note in his book that Harold left his residence and noted the time at 11:55 PM.

He stayed behind Harold as he drove hoping he didn't notice he had a tail. So far, Harold never looked twice at the white car always behind him.

"Oh shit," the PI said when he saw where Harold stopped. He grabbed his cell and called Gary. The call woke him and he finally found the phone.

"Harold is parked in front of your apartment. What are my orders?"

That brought Gary fully awake and he sat up. Sarah heard and ran to the light switch.

"Watch and see what he does," Gary said. "Stay on the phone with me."

"He's leaving," the PI reported.

"Stay on his tail, but be careful, it will be easier for him to spot you at night."

"I know," the PI replied. "He went around the corner. I can see his tail lights."

"He turned into the alley, and stopped behind your

126

apartment. There's enough light for me to see from the streetlights and moon. He's walking to your back door."

"If he breaks in, call the police and report it. Stay out of sight and tell me what happens."

"Harold broke the back glass with his elbow and is inside," the PI reported. I'm calling the police. I'll call you back after I report the break in."

Gary closed the phone and welcomed Sarah into his arms to wait. She was standing close and heard.

His phone rang in less than a minute. "Harold is still inside; the police are on the way."

"Move away, but where you can see and stay on the phone. Let them handle it."

"The police have arrived, one car in front and one behind. They have Harold trapped inside. Harold just ran out the back door and is running toward his car. Two policemen are waiting behind their car."

Gary and Sarah heard gunshots. She screamed and clutched Gary.

"One policeman is down," the PI said. "The other is helping his wounded partner. Harold made it to his car and is racing away. The police car that was in front is in pursuit."

"Go home," Gary said. "You did an outstanding job. When you learn more, let me know. Find out the condition of the policeman, and if they caught Harold, call, regardless of the time."

"Yes sir," he said and the phone went dead.

He held Sarah in his arms and kissed her nose. The expression on her face was awful. She looked up with teary eyes. "Harold shot a policeman," she said.

"I know. The alcohol has pickled his brain and he's lost all sense of reality. He would have killed you if given the chance. How that he has crossed the line, it was only a matter of time. The police will get him. Shooting a cop will have every law enforcement agency in the area on alert for him."

A shiver went down her spine at that thought. "Harold will kill you if given the chance," she said. "If he's not caught, he could be waiting for you in town. I don't want you to go back on Tuesday. He could shoot you on sight. I know he has a deer rifle. I heard him brag he killed a deer at 400 yards."

"Until he's caught, I'm staying here. Now that he knows you're with me, he may come here. Finding my ranch wouldn't be that difficult, but getting to our home would not be impossible. He might buy a GPS."

Sleep was not out of the question for them now. She pulled a robe on and he put on shorts and they went to the den. She made coffee and they sat at the bar waiting.

It was after two AM when the PI called.
"The policeman died. Harold escaped, but they know his identity. Every cop in the area is looking for him. He won't get far."

"Thanks," Gary said. "Keep me posted."

"We may as well go back to bed," she said. "We may not sleep, but I can lie in your arms where it's warm and comfortable."

She settled into her place and put her hand on his chest. "How fast can he get here? I mean, when do I have to start worrying, big time?"

"At the earliest, it would be morning. I'll warn Juan, Sam and Brock to be on the lookout for a strange car."

"I shot a pistol when I was younger," she said. "My dad taught me. Do you have one I can carry? As a precaution, in case he comes here."

Gary rolled from the bed and went to his office and came back with a .38 revolver. She reached for it and aimed at the wall. "Perfect," she said. "Is it loaded?"

"Yes, and empty gun is worthless. Tomorrow morning, I want you to fire is several time, to get the hang of it. When I'm gone, I want you to keep it close. Everybody does."

"I can do that, will you buy me a holster."

He nodded. "And you need good riding boots. We'll go into town as soon as possible. Sarah, at times I can't believe how lucky I was to meet you. It seems we were made for each other."

She put her new pistol on the table beside the bed and rolled under him.

***

The sun was just peaking over the ridge east of the ranch house when Gary left the bed. He tried not to wake her, but she pushed up and saw him going to the bathroom. She hurried to the kitchen to make fresh coffee.

He was dressed when he came to the kitchen. She poured him a cup, and he took a couple of sips. "I'm going to talk to the men before they leave." He took the cup with him.

When he came back, she had his breakfast ready, but before he could sit, she put her arms around his neck. "I'm sorry I got you into this. If anything happened to you, I couldn't stand it. I said this before, but after what Harold did last night. I can see him shooting on sight now; he has nothing more to lose. I'm going to go someplace away from here and let him know I'm not with you. That way, he won't come here and possibly kill you. If you kill him, you would be in trouble. I love you too much to take the chance of anything happening to you because of me."

She turned and ran toward the bedroom with tears flowing.

He caught her before she got out of the room and lifted her into his arms and carried her to the recliner and sat with her in his lap.

His voice was as sharp as she had ever heard. "Sarah, damn it. Listen to me and hear every word I say. I mean it. If you ever leave me, it will not be for that reason. I signed on for the duration, for better or worse. This is our problem, ours, not yours. If I hadn't come into your life it would have only postponed the inevitable for a short time. Harold was on a collision course with disaster. Alcohol was working on his brain and he was going to snap. Something would have triggered it, regardless of what you did."

"Are you listening to me?" he asked.

"Yes, of course I am," she managed.

"When we confronted him at the bank, he exploded and threw a chair at us, and then kicked the door down in my office. If he had a gun, he would have started shooting at us, or anybody in the building. The man is crazy, paranoid. He's using you as an excuse to slash out at society."

"There's no way to stop him now. He has killed and has the taste for it. He'll attempt to kill again; it may be me or us. It could be another policeman, or a clerk in a convenience store that says something wrong. If the police don't kill him, he'll be placed in prison for the criminally insane."

"As I said, this is our problem, and we'll face it side by side. Now let's eat breakfast and your shooting lessons are about to start. Should Harold come here, I want you prepared."

"I couldn't kill him," she whimpered. "He may be crazy, but he's also sick. I would shoot his legs or arm, but I couldn't shoot him in the heart or head."

"Darling, if you're placed in that position, kill or be killed, aim at the center of his chest, and pull the damn trigger. Do you hear me? He'll kill you without hesitation."

"I hear you, but I'm not sure I could."

"The odds of you being in that position are high, but I'm not taking the chance. We, not you, are getting out of here. If that bastard kills you, I don't want to live without you."

He helped her stand. "Go dress and pack a few things for both of us. I have things to do before we leave."

He was reaching for the phone when she raced toward the bedroom. She knew he meant what he said. She wouldn't want to live without him now.

Gary called the sheriff's office. "Sheriff Maxwell," Gary said. "This is Gary Justice, have you heard about the shooting where a policeman was killed last night?"

"Yes, I'm following it. In fact, I have my deputies on the highway looking for the vehicle."

"The man that did the shooting was Harold Nance," Gary Said. "He's on his way to kill me. He's an employee at my bank. When we confronted him with his drinking problem, he exploded and became violent. The police were called to my apartment in town last night when it was reported somebody was breaking in, that is where the policeman was killed. Harold was after me."

There was silence on the line for a few moments.

"Where are you now?" Sheriff Maxwell asked.

"At the ranch. I warned Juan, Sam and Brock to be on the lookout for a strange car, but I don't want them involved. Harold is armed with a pistol and deer rifle. I was told he's a crack shot. Since he has already killed a policeman, he has nothing more to lose, another killing won't matter."

"What are you going to do?" the sheriff asked.

"Sarah Nance is with me, we're going to leave and hide out until he's arrested. I hate to run, but under the circumstances, it's the prudent thing to do."

"Sarah Nance is with you?" Maxwell asked. "Is she his wife?"

"Yes, they're separated and she's filing for divorce. That is another reason he is after me and her, he's insanely jealous."

"I see," Maxwell said, "and that's why he's coming here, to kill you and her."

"That's the way I have it figured. He went to my apartment for that purpose expecting us to be there. When I wasn't there, it only makes sense he's coming here. He can obtain the directions to the ranch without too much difficulty."

"I'll have a deputy stationed on the road to your ranch. Hopefully, if your right, we can stop him there without bloodshed."

"Thanks," Gary said. "Caution your deputy to be cautious, I read Harold as a back shooter." He hurried to help Sarah pack. He found her dressed and putting clothes in a bag. He helped and reached for the bag and her hand and they went out the door. Juan was walking toward them.

"Juan," Gary said. "The sheriff has been alerted. I suggest you take Maria somewhere and tell Brock and Sam to do the same. I don't want any of you hurt. I'm taking Sarah some place safe until this is over. I don't want her hurt."

"I'll send Maria to visit her mother and Brock and Sam have already gone to the pasture. They both had their saddle guns. They'll be okay with that city tenderfoot. Besides, they were headed to the windmill on the hill. There's no way a stranger could find it, and there would be no reason for

131

anybody to go there without a reason."

"If Maria goes to her mom's what about you. I don't want you here. Nance is crazy and out of control. He might shoot you or sight, or abduct you to learn where we went."

"I'm not going to run. If he comes here and nobody is here, he may burn us out for spite. I'll be in the barn, and have my shotgun loaded with buckshot."

"Juan, I don't want you involved. If you shoot the bastard, you could be in trouble. With the bleeding heart idiots we have, they could file on you for murder, or manslaughter. That's the reason I am getting Sarah away from here. I would like to put one through Harold' forehead."

"Go get Maria and go with her today. I'll call when it's safe to come back."

"You're the boss," Juan said and turned to go to his house.

Sarah was already in his car waiting. He jumped in and drove toward the highway. "How for is it to the highway," she asked.

"About 10 miles and 6 of that is a dirt private road."

"What does that mean?" she asked.

"It belongs to us."

"What do you mean, belongs to us?"

"It's on our ranch. That's why I said it would be hard for Harold to find our ranch house, but using a GPS, it would be possible, I suppose."

"Just how big is the ranch?" she asked.

"Do you know how many acres is in a section?" he asked.

"Six hundred and forty, a section is one mile square."

"Very good," he teased, "for a school teacher." He was hoping to keep their conversation light.

"So in sections, how many in the ranch?" she asked.

"Forty-two," he replied, keeping his eyes on the narrow dirt road.

She gasped, mentally calculating. "That's almost 27 thousand acres," she said.

He nodded. "Our kids will have plenty of room to play

outside."

She had to laugh at that.

"There may be trouble ahead," he said.

He pulled his pistol and placed it on the dash in front of him where it would be easy to reach. "Where is your weapon?" he asked.

She reached for it in her pocket and held it in her lap. "I see two cars in front of us," she said. "One is a police car. I see the lights on top."

He slowed and leaned forward to see better. "I don't see anybody moving around," he said.

Suddenly, a bullet shattered the windshield and ripped through his left arm below the shoulder.

Gary frantically turned the wheel to the right to shield Sarah from the shooter. The car skidded, but held and made the ninety degree circle and sped back the way they came leaving a cloud of dust.

As soon as they went over a small hill he braked to a stop. "Take the wheel, I need to stop the flow of blood," he said. She didn't panic seeing blood gushing from his arm. She opened her door and jumped out and ran around to his side and helped Gary out of the car and around to the passenger side. When he was inside, she closed the door and went to the driver's side and gave the car gas.

She glanced his way and he was working to tie his handkerchief around his arm to stop the flow of blood. "Can I help?" she asked.

"I can manage, just drive. Harold may be following. Can you see him behind us?"

Sarah glanced in the mirror. "A car is following," she said.

She looked at his arm and saw the flow of blood had slowed dramatically, but it was still dripping. Gary pulled his cell and looked for Sheriff Maxwell's number.

"This is Gary Justice. We were on the way to the highway and saw one of your cars and another stopped in the middle of the road. When we got close, somebody fired at us. He got me in my left arm. We turned around, but he's following us."

"Where are you?" Maxwell asked.

"We were at the intersection where my road meets the county road."

"Did you see my deputy?" the lawman asked.

"No, we were about a quarter mile away when we were fired on."

"How bad are you wounded?"

"The bullet went through my arm below the shoulder. I have almost stopped the blood flow with compression. Sarah is driving now. We're driving back toward my home, but the car behind is gaining on us. Sarah isn't accustomed to driving on ranch roads."

"I'm about ten minutes from the intersection. Another deputy is in front of me and will stop to check on the deputy. I'll be behind you and driving as fast as I can." Gary ended the call.

"He's closing fast," Sarah said.

"Slow a little and take the next left," Gary said. "It's another ranch road and much rougher. I wish we were in my truck."

Sarah made the turn even though the car tried to fishtail. She handled it and straightened out without losing control. "Great job," he said.

"Where are we going?" she asked as she avoided rocks and clumps of brush.

"Damn," Gary said," "he made the turn with us. We're going to the mill on the hill. That's where Sam and Brock are working."

He found Sam's name in his cell and punched the talk button. He let it ring until it went to voice mail. He found Brock and called. The same, no answer.

"They're probably on the tower and can't hear their phone."

Sarah drove as fast as she dared. She didn't want to hit a rock or a clump of bush and disable the car. Harold would catch them.

She glanced at Gary and he lay with his head back on the seat. "Gary, Gary," she shouted. He didn't reply. She reached over and shook him. He fell against the door and she knew he was unconscious. She screamed, but kept driving. A windmill appeared when she went over a hill and she saw a truck parked beside the tower.

She hit the horn and held it until she saw two men scrambling down the ladder.

She slid to a stop behind their truck and saw both of the cowboys grabbing their saddle guns and take position behind the truck. They saw the tailing car and suspected the reason.

Harold slid to a stop and turned his car to the side. He jumped out and aimed the deer rifle at the work truck of the two cowboys. Sarah raced around and opened the door on Gary's side. She caught him and kept him from falling to the ground. His weight pulled her down saving her life. A bullet tore into the car where her head had been.

The two cowboys returned fire, but Harold was behind his car with the motor between them. Harold jacked in another bullet and took his time and aimed. His next shot took the hat from Brock and sent it sailing, but he didn't draw blood.

Sarah screamed when she saw the pale face of Gary. She checked his eyes and knew he was in serious trouble. She scrambled to where the two cowboys were crouched. Gary was shot and is dying unless we get him help. The sheriff is less than ten minutes from here, but I don't know if Gary can last that long. He lost so much blood and is still bleeding."

"We can't get a shot, and that bastard is good," Brock said. "He got my hat and only the top was showing above the hood of the truck. Can you shoot a rifle?" he asked.

"Yes, I've shot some, but I probably couldn't hit him."

Brock handed her the rifle, don't let him get a shot at you, but you two can stall him until the sheriff comes in behind him."

Gary's phone rang. Brock scrambled and found it on his belt. "This is Sheriff Maxwell, where are you?"

Sheriff, this is Brock, we're at the mill on the hill, where are you?"

"Damn if I know, on the road to your ranch house, but I can't see anybody in front of me. I do see a water tank

135

coming up on my right. A lot of cattails are growing along the sides."

"I know where you are," Brock said. "Take the next left, but look close. It's hard to see, about a quarter mile from where you are. Hurry, Gary is unconscious."

"I'll call for a medical helicopter," Maxwell said.

Brock bent over Gary and looked at the soaked bandage. He removed it and saw a severed vein. He reached into the wound and clamped it with his fingers."

Harold changed positions behind his car after every shot. They never knew where to look for him. He would pop up and shoot and be gone before they could sight in on him. Sam and Sarah were afraid to show any part of their body. Harold was too good with the rifle.

"Sarah, I need your help," Brock said. "Sam can you hold him off?"

"For now, he's taking pot shots at us, but not attempting to rush us. Hopefully Maxwell will get here soon before he gets lucky."

Sarah scrambled back to Brock. He was still holding the vein with his fingers. I need something to clamp this," he said. "Would you have a hairpin?"

She found her purse in the car and fished around, but then dumped the contents on the floorboard and searched. She crawled back to Brock with a hairpin in her hand.

"Help me," Brock said. "I'm going to pull the vein out enough for you to clamp the hairpin on it to stop the blood loss."

She did as he asked and when he released the vein, there was no blood. "Good job," Brock said. "Sit here with his head in your lap and talk to him. He can hear you even unconscious. Tell him you want and need him and to stay with us for a few more minutes."

She did as he requested and started to talk, optimistic he would hear. Gary's eyes moved behind his eyelids and she hoped that was a good sign.

Brock moved back to the truck and took his position. "What's he doing?"

"He hasn't shot in a while," Sam said. "I haven't seen

any movement."

Brock instantly shifted to look to the sides. "He's trying to flank us. From the other side of his car he could have made it to the trees and is moving to get a clear shot at us. You watch to the left and I'll have the right covered."

Both men shifted to cover the most likely places Harold would attempt an ambush. Brock saw movements in the bushes and squeezed off a round for effect.

They heard thrashing in the bushes. Sam belly crawled to the side of Gary's car for a better angle at where they suspected Harold would be.

A shot from a hidden location in the rocks caused both men to duck down. "Where did that round go?" Brock asked. "I heard it hit metal, but it wasn't close to me."

"Me neither," Sam said.

"Shit," Brock shouted. "Drag Gary to the windmill. I'll cover you. That bastard shot our gas tank. I see gasoline running out on the ground. He intends to blow us up."

Another shot punctured the tank on Gary's car. Brock was trying to locate the shooter, but could see nothing. He glanced over his shoulder and saw Sarah and Sam pulling Gary to the base of the windmill. Thankfully, Gary's car offered some protection from Harold.

The tower didn't offer much protection, but it would be better than being between the two vehicles if the gas was ignited. Brock moved backward on his knees, keeping his rifle aimed if he got a shot.

A bullet tore through his shirt sleeve, but didn't draw blood. Another bullet plowed into the ground a foot in front of him.

He saw gun slight, aimed and fired. Harold grunted, but Brock didn't think he scored a hit, but hopefully the shot was close enough to keep Harold from taking time to sight in on them.

The sound of a siren caused everybody to look toward the sound. The light bar was flashing as the police car raced toward them. "Finally," Sam said.

"Don't give him a target; it won't be over until that bastard is buzzard bait."

Too prove his point, a bullet tore a chunk from the windmill tower only six inches from Sam's ear. He dove and covered both Sarah and Gary with his body. Brock fired where he thought the shot came from.

Sam was covering the Sarah and Gary, but was looking as well. "I see him running toward his car," he shouted.

Brock rolled into a better shooting position and systematically put a round in each tire. "He's not going to escape in that car," he said.

Sheriff Maxwell stepped from his car and took cover behind his door. "Give it up Nance," he yelled.

"Fuck you," Nance shouted. "I ain't sitting in a jail cell for years facing no fucking needle in my arm." He began to fire at the sheriff as fast as he could bolt in fresh bullets.

"Maxwell waited until the rifle was out of ammunition, and stood up and aimed. His first bullet took Nance above the belt buckle, but each succeeding bullet worked its way up until the last knocked Harold on his back with a hole between his eyes.

"It's over," Maxwell shouted. He ran to the supine man and picked up the rifle and jerked the pistol from his belt. He hurried to where Gary lay with his head in Sarah's lap. "How is he?"

"Alive, thanks to Brock," she said. "He stopped the bleeding, but I hope the helicopter gets here soon."

Brock pointed and shouted. "There it is, but he is too far north."

He scrambled up the windmill tower and stood on the top table and waved his shirt. The helicopter made a quick turn and then set down close to them.

Two paramedics scrambled out and raced to Gary. They quickly had him packaged and on a gurney. An IV was inserted into his arm. "Can I ride with him?" she asked.

She didn't wait for a reply, and ran to the helicopter and was inside to help them load Gary.

Chapter 13

Sarah was seated in the waiting room when Sheriff Maxwell came in and sat beside her. "I was given a report on Gary's condition," she said. "He's going to recover fully. He lost blood, but he's young and strong. A lot of TLC and good ranch cooked steak and he'll be up and rearing to go in a few days. And, I'll make sure he gets plenty of both. How is your deputy? I heard they had to do extensive surgery on him."

"Like Gary, he'll recover, but it'll take significantly more time. The bullets did a lot of damage to the muscles in his shoulder and back. Harold drove to the deputy's car and started shooting before he said a word."

Maxwell stood with his hat in his hand. "I was on the way to visit him when I saw you. I understand you're going to marry Gary and live here."

"That's our plan," she said with her first smile. "We want a family and this appears a good place to raise kids."

"It is. Nothing exciting ever happens."

"Really," she said with a hardy chuckle. "If what happened this morning wasn't exciting, then I don't want to be around when something exciting happens."

"That was the exception to the rule," Maxwell said.

"You know Brock saved his life," she said. "That's what the doctor told me. I'm glad he was there and knew what to do. I didn't."

"Brock was a medic in the military," he said.

A nurse came to them. "Sarah, Gary is asking for you. The doctor said you can see him now, he's been moved to a room and alert. I'll take you."

Sheriff Maxwell followed them.

The nurse almost had to run to keep up with Sarah. She found Gary waiting with his good arm open. The other was in a cast.

Her tears of joy streaked her face as she melted into his embrace. The nurse and Sheriff Maxwell stood at the door watching the happy couple.

"They'll make a welcome addition to our community," she said.

As soon as Sarah stood, Sheriff Maxwell walked to the bed. "Gary, I'm happy to see you looking so good. You were as pale as a ghost yesterday at the mill on the hill."

"I was told you got Harold," Gary said.

Maxwell nodded. "When we took Harold's body into town, I searched it. I found this in his pocket."

He handed Gary a large envelope with Cyprus State Bank printed on the outside. Gary opened it and saw the envelope stuffed with money.

"Over half a million," Maxwell said. "I have to keep it until the hearing. Evidence, you understand. But I wanted you to know. I can only think of one place it came from, your bank."

Gary nodded and handed the envelope back to Maxwell. "Thanks, I'll order an audit tomorrow."

Maxwell put the envelope in his pocket and backed from the room. "I'll leave you two for some privacy." He closed the door and Sarah leaned over for a long kiss.

When she stood up, she met his face and smiled.

"Yes," she said.

He let out a whoop that could be heard throughout the hospital.